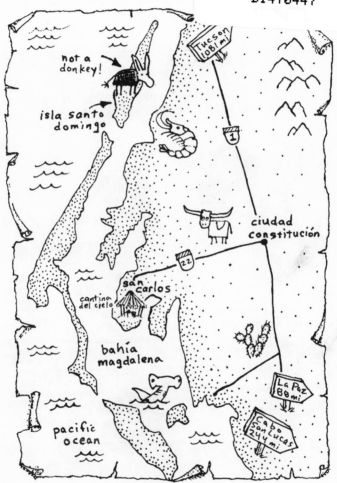

Fish's map of the habitable universe

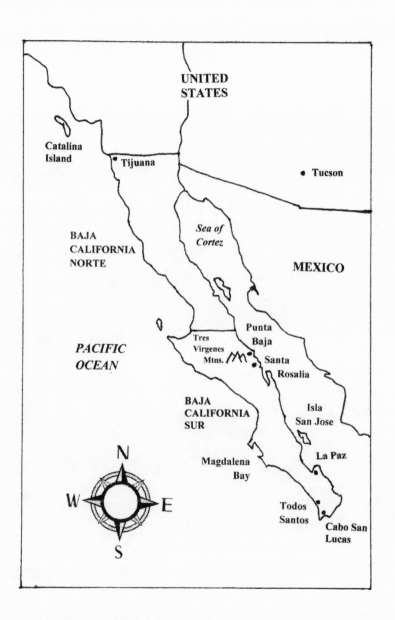

THE
CROOKED
PEARL

THE CROOKED PEARL

SHAUN MOREY

THOMAS & MERCER

Text copyright © 2013 Shaun Morey

Printed in the United States of America.

Published by Thomas & Mercer, Seattle

www.apub.com

ISBN-13: 9781612184999
ISBN-10: 1612184995
LCCN: 2013906099

This one's for Maggie.

Rich are the sea-gods . . . [who] grope the sea for pearls.

—Ralph Waldo Emerson

CHAPTER ONE

San Evaristo, Baja California Sur

The boy awoke at dawn and watched his grandfather shuffle across the dirt floor to the glassless window. The sound of crashing waves resonated through the thin-walled shack, and the boy watched the old man part the potato-sack curtains and gaze out at the pale sky. Tucked beneath his Mexican blanket, he hoped his grandfather would put away his work clothes and return to his own cot in the corner with its meager pillow and matching blanket.

Despite their daily hand-washing, the old man's clothes betrayed a life at sea. Blood from untold fish, bile, and bits of viscera marked indelible patterns of death across the threadbare cloth, telltale signs of the life-and-death struggles that permanently stained the old man's mahogany skin. Even in the dim light, the boy could see scars of battle on his grandfather's thick and twisted fingers. Adolfo Ruiz Zaragosa, the *pueblita's* most senior *pangero*, had spent six decades dropping handlines and setting nets, and despite the boy's fears, today would be no different.

Zaragosa paused at a rickety pantry and removed a corn tortilla, his head cocked to gauge another gust of wind. Far to the east, storm clouds clustered like gray fists bruising the surface of an aubergine sea. Along the shore, gulls huddled in sullen packs, their webbed feet fidgeting against the stinging sand, their beaks tucked low. Overhead, arch-backed palms rattled their fronds like bones of the dead.

The boy sat up. "Please, *Abuelo*. The sky is angry today."

"Listen to the wind, *Nieto*," Zaragosa said, filling the tortilla with *machaca con chile* and rolling it tightly, then cinching it inside a blanket of foil. "It stirs the air, but it blows from the mountains. The storm will follow and pass us far to the south."

Through the window, the boy could see the humpbacked waves crash across the seawall. The biggest waves shook the shack, and the boy flinched with every cresting swell, his eyes widening at the riot of foam. He stood up from the small straw mattress and crossed to the shack's door, an opening covered by more potato sacks sewn together, and looked toward the faint reddish glow on the horizon.

"The color of the sky. It scares me."

Zaragosa dropped the burrito, a mango, and a container of water into a plastic yellow bag, the kind the local *tienda* used for groceries. Such bags, so often carelessly discarded, always seemed to find the thorny branches of palo verde trees and palo Adans and mesquites that grew along the southern Baja California coastline. Zaragosa patted the boy on the shoulder.

"It is good to know fear, Manolín. Many of my *compadres* did not, and they no longer share the sea with me."

"But the fish will hide if the sea is rough."

"Perhaps." Zaragosa's smile lifted his heavy gray beard. "But I know their secrets. And I will set my nets early so that after school I can take you to the market for ice cream. *Fresa con caramelo, no?*"

Manolín hugged his grandfather.

"Promise me you will learn something new today and teach me when I return."

"I promise," Manolín said.

Zaragosa shuffled through the opening and into the familiar murk of dawn. He felt the briny mist from the waves and smelled the seaweed forced ashore in great clumps. His senses took in the kelp paddies decomposing into nutrient-rich homes for the sea lice and sand fleas and the armies of blue crabs that patrolled the beach at night. Zaragosa stepped around a fresh mound of kelp and felt the thimble-sized husks crush beneath his feet. The roving sandpipers and tattlers had pecked clean the soft-shelled crustaceans. Above him, a pair of seagulls screeched and wheeled into the rising wind. A lone sea lion barked in the distance.

With his lunch looped around a crooked finger and slung across his shoulder, Zaragosa approached the makeshift marina where his *panga* lay anchored in the shallows. He boarded the small canoe-shaped boat and motored toward Isla San Jose, a mountainous island fifteen miles from the village. The wind had not subsided, and waves slapped against the *panga*'s hull, forming wings of mist that flew across the bow. An hour later, as the sun climbed a wall of dark cumulous clouds, Zaragosa set his net near the cactus-strewn island, then creased an empty potato sack and wrapped it around his neck like a shawl.

For three hours he hauled the old net but managed only a handful of mullet and two small stingrays that he released unharmed. Moving around the island, he found a lee from the wind near some cliffs and a small beach, and there he ate his lunch. The sun had risen above the clouds now, and the wind blew fiercely out beyond the lee; but the storm was moving toward the mountains like he'd told his grandson, and he crossed himself, giving thanks to La Virgen de Guadalupe.

He drank sparingly from his water jug and glanced out at the whitecapped sea, surprised that the other *pangeros* had not yet fanned across the horizon. But the roiling waves made viewing difficult, and his eyes were not as keen anymore. He studied the calmer water at the edge of the lee and noticed a slight discoloration near the current break. It was a shallow reef not much more than a soccer field from the island. As he set his net over the mossy shadows of coral and rock, he crossed himself again. It had been years since he'd fished so close to shore, preferring the deeper seamounts and rising banks where the giant trevally and schooling yellowtail massed as though beckoned to a great feast.

He dozed for an hour and, when he awoke, the sun had slipped behind a thick canvas of clouds. He hauled the net. It was empty but for some sea grass and a small eel that wriggled free and threaded the water like a lost necklace. But then the last of the nylon netting came over the transom with a clunk, and Zaragosa looked down to see a softball-sized shell covered in barnacles. His tired eyes widened, and he quickly untangled the catch, cradling it in his hands like something fragile.

"*Gracias Dios,*" he muttered, and kissed the prize, setting it gently to the thwart.

Pearl oysters were thought extinct in the Sea of Cortez, decimated centuries ago by the greedy Spaniards and their fleets of deadly galleons. But a few beds remained, protected by the ghost of Mechudo, the young diver drowned in the jaws of a giant oyster. Zaragosa had heard the legend as a boy—how the young diver refused to bequeath the first pearl to the church and how this breach from custom forever haunted the waters of La Paz Bay. As a young man, Zaragosa had dreamed of restoring honor to the old custom; but the famed oyster beds had vanished, and his search for pearls was replaced by the day-to-day demands of handlining and gill netting.

Now, as Zaragosa reached into his bucket of rusty tools to remove a heavy knife, the memories rushed back, and his heart began to race. He shucked the enormous oyster, and his jaw hinged open. The innards revealed more than gray-lipped flesh. Ensconced on its slippery throne was an orb as pale and dull as the tourists from the north. Zaragosa knew the large pearl, the size of a cowrie shell, was worth a boatload of fish, especially when set in sterling silver and presented to the gringos at the tourist shops in La Paz.

But this pearl was not destined for the market. After so many decades, the wrongs of Mechudo would at last be righted, the old curse lifted by his unlikely snag of an oyster whose pearl was now destined for holiness.

Zaragosa said a silent prayer, and as he plucked the prize from its cradle, the sun squeezed through a break in the clouds and exposed the true soul of the margarite. There, beneath the skin of hardened mucus, was a blush of amethyst so astonishing that it blurred the old man's gaze. He held the jewel to the sky and slumped to his knees. Emotion dampened his beard and swelled his heart. An oyster bed that produced purple-hued pearls of such size was more than rare. It was a lifetime of hauling nets and gutting fish. It was a small house with a thatched roof. It was security for Manolín, whose mother lay buried in the small hillside cemetery, and whose father had fled north, never to return.

Zaragosa placed the pearl inside the foil from lunch and dropped it into the plastic yellow bag, tying the handles tightly. He wedged the bag beneath the bow and stood to survey the stretch of shallow green water. Where one pearl took root, others would seed. He rummaged beneath the starboard gunwale and removed a secondhand mask. Cracked and without a snorkel, the faceplate allowed a brief window to the underworld, and within an hour Zaragosa had filled the gunnysack with prized shellfish.

He grabbed the knife and shucked a dozen oysters in less than a minute, tossing the split shells into a second gunnysack for dinner. He freed a thirteenth oyster from the sack, pressed the blade into the seam, and torqued his wrist. The oyster opened, and he glimpsed a spot of violet. His breath caught in his throat.

Carefully, he unfolded the hinged shells and lifted the pearl free. Again he dropped to his knees and gave thanks before adding the pearl to the tinfoil. Then he returned to the bag of oysters and ten minutes later added a third pearl to his collection.

This one was the largest of the three, lopsided, but with a bloom of rose at its center. A trancelike state descended over him as he swiftly shucked the remaining oysters. The years of toil dropped away, and the future, once so bleak, now glowed with promise. Rather than glance at the horizon or the changing sky above, his tired brown eyes focused on the green water and the prolific reef beneath the waves.

"*Uno más,*" he wheezed. "*Por todos santos del mundo.*"

Zaragosa swam hard, past the shallow tier of sand to the sloping underwater ledge where sunlight dimmed and predators roamed. Unafraid, he kicked until his lungs ached. The dive mask tightened against his face, and his ears begged for forgiveness. Shadows of unconsciousness swam sharklike in his vision. And then he saw it: a mollusk of matronly proportions, a shellfish as voluptuous as a señora in a Diego Rivera painting.

Zaragosa grabbed the bivalve with both hands and tugged it free. Turning, he walked more than swam up the murky slope. He dropped the shell in the shallows and kicked to the surface, gasping for air. It took him two more dives to lug the oyster to the *panga.*

Lying on his back to catch his breath, he at last noticed the purple clouds churning overhead, their swollen bellies writhing with static as if unborn beasts bucked for freedom. Beneath him he could feel the strengthening of the waves against the hull.

"Mechudo," he uttered the cursed name, and quickly pulled anchor and started the outboard engine.

The waves had breached the lee and were rolling across the bay like untethered cordwood. He turned the narrow boat into the risers to avoid foundering and heard the engine strain. The bow buried into a breaking wave, and Zaragosa gunned the throttle. Water rushed over the gunwales. The *panga* porpoised through a heavy lip of water and dropped precipitously into the descending trough.

Zaragosa bailed frantically with one hand while steering the outboard with the other. He rode the face of another wave, spyhopped over the crest, and rounded the corner of the island. His soul sank at the sight of a rabid sea. Roiling water avalanched down mountainous swells. Bales of foam stampeded across the channel, blurring the coastline and his village of San Evaristo.

Lightning crackled and rain began to fall, and as Zaragosa spun the boat back toward the relative safety of the reef, a colossal wave reared overhead like the white-tipped finger of God. For an instant Zaragosa thought the wave might demand repentance for his foolishness. Instead, the *panga* jackknifed, and Zaragosa lost his balance and fell to the floorboards. He heard a sickening crack. Pain lanced through his arm. He gripped the edge of the *panga* and gaped at the awkward bend of his elbow.

A second wave slammed the *panga,* and the gunnysack tore open, raining oysters upon him, broken shells slicing into his face and across his hands. Salt water washing over the transom freed the yellow bag from beneath the bow. Zaragosa reached out desperately for it with his good arm; but then the bow spun and the stern dropped, and he was weightless, and then swimming.

The island was less than a soccer field away, yet it seemed like hours before the beach loomed like a sandy fist. Levees of salt water lifted him into the sky. He backpedaled, hoping for a break in the swells, but the sets were unrelenting and Zaragosa soon hurtled uncontrollably down a hunchbacked wave.

Sand crushed his ribs and split his nose. His working hand dug into the beach, furrowing the heavy sand like a faulty plow. He pedaled his feet and felt brief traction beneath his toes. Drenching spray stung his eyes. Sea foam choked his lungs. As he scrambled up the cascading shoreline, a second mountainous wave caught his legs and dragged him back to sea, the roar of water clapping his ears like a palmed hand.

Through the mist of the shattered wave he saw a rosy stain marking his backward path. The blood looked beautiful in the stormy light, as if death approached more like an angel than a devil. The sea sucked him down, but the thought of heavenly spirits lifted Zaragosa's thick gray whiskers and softened a face landscaped in time.

Then another comber steamrolled toward the beach, and Zaragosa felt himself heaved upward again, his body airborne on the breaking wave. He sucked at the swirling air and rolled sideways at the sudden drop like a man flung from a moving cliff. His good arm covered his head while the other, crooked and swollen, sailed uselessly beside him.

The explosion of seawater rocketed the breath from his lungs. He crumpled to the sand, rolled to his knees, and struggled forward inch by inch. A lifetime hauling nets had prepared him for such a trial. Perseverance was the seaman's mantra, and Zaragosa bore the scars of his homage across his skin; scars that gave him hope in the grip of a world-class maelstrom.

The wash of water drained past him like a miner's sieve, and as the air returned to his lungs, Zaragosa burrowed his good hand wrist-deep into the sand. He thought of Manolín and of the lavender pearls. He thought of the one he had prayed over, had given thanks to, had offered to La Virgen de Guadalupe. He thought of the others entombed in the yellow bag as if nothing but flotsam on a slashing sea.

"*Lo siento, niño,*" he muttered as tears streamed down his face.

Again he was pulled into the sea, and again the water slammed him to the beach. Time slowed and his vision clouded, but still Zaragosa fought on. He fought for Manolín and for the riches he knew were hidden in the reef beneath the storm, and then he was lifted into a wave of unimaginable height. As it crested skyward, though, the surge of water paused. A second wave had undercut the first and cushioned Zaragosa's fall. He clawed at the sand and crabbed once more toward safety. He advanced up the slope, praying for the embankment to hold, pleading for the storm to subside.

He had just reached for another anchor of sand when the island itself began to tremble like an immense beast preparing to rise to its feet. The beach began to give way. The quaking grew yet more violent, knocking Zaragosa flat to the ground. Rock slides melted the steep cliffs above him, shearing tree-sized cacti from their footings. Zaragosa rolled sideways along the shore, grimacing each time he fell across his broken arm. As the crush of debris slid by, the earthquake weakened and the land fell eerily silent.

Zaragosa clambered to his knees. He had just crossed himself when he heard the howl of water gathering behind him.

Life be damned if it thought him a coward. Death be damned if it thought him a traitor.

"Diablo!" he screamed, and turned to face down the angry sea.

But instead of approaching, the waves were retreating, as if drawn by some unthinkable force. Adrenaline surged through Zaragosa. Sculling one-armed toward the safety of the cliff, he reached the littoral without looking back and staggered into the fallen rocks. He knew the waves were regrouping, knew the earthquake that shook the island had also angered the sea, awakening a demon wall of water.

Zaragosa knew to survive he had to climb.

The rock slides had loosened the shale, and twice the old man fell painfully to the rubble. But the rain had stopped and the sky had brightened, and thoughts of his grandson renewed his strength. Within minutes Zaragosa had reached the base of the first summit. He glanced back at the ocean and felt a sickness rise through his body. An immense bulge of water was fast approaching, its surface rolling toward him like an angry serpent. Zaragosa peered up at the thirty feet of cactus-strewn boulders that blocked his way to the top. He turned again toward the tsunami and swallowed dryly.

"Dios mío," he sputtered, and began to scramble over the spiked terrain.

Halfway up, he collapsed, gasping for breath between boulders, the thick calluses of his feet bloody and pincushioned with thorns. The bedrock shuddered beneath him, and Zaragosa glanced down. The sea had exploded against the island and was surging up the shoreline.

The old man willed himself deeper into the crevices and watched the rising mass of water infest the hillside like a plague. Columns of seawater smothered everything. The gargantuan wave swarmed over low-lying scrub, knocking boulders like tenpins. It swallowed cacti and slag, and tore the cliff face below to confetti.

Zaragosa closed his eyes. He raised his thumb and forefinger to his forehead, then lowered both to his heart. He raised them to his left shoulder, and then to his right. He muttered a prayer and opened his eyes—and caught sight of the yellow bag, sliding past in a sweeping current just beneath him and then vanishing around the bend of the island.

He knew it was a sign—a reminder of an old man's folly, a greed that had once again awakened the ghost of Mechudo.

When Zaragosa looked below him again, he found the rising sea spreading its Herculean wings. He felt the water at his feet, his calves, his thighs. He closed his eyes. The water flowed over his waist, and he heard the adjacent boulders creak. The sea had begun to lift him, pulling him into the collapsing hillside, when abruptly it stopped. The old man opened his eyes and watched the sea retreat down the broken terrain, a river of detritus following in its wake.

"Madre de Dios," Zaragosa muttered, then dropped his face to his chest and wept.

CHAPTER TWO

Puerto San Carlos, Baja California Sur

One week after the earthquake shook much of southern Baja, Atticus Fish returned to his daily predawn ride aboard his Appaloosa mule, Mephistopheles. He wore a pair of lightweight sailcloth pants and a white Guayabera shirt open to the waist. A homemade fish-skin cap covered the sun-bleached locks that fell to his wide shoulders. He wore no shoes and carried a sheathed machete tied to the thigh of his loose-fitting pants.

Over the last few days he'd repaired the minor damage the earthquake caused his bar/restaurant, Cantina del Cielo, and helped the handful of businesses in the nearby town of Puerto San Carlos reopen. He'd also finalized his offer—in partnership with the Nature Conservancy—to purchase the chain of barrier islands protecting his beloved Magdalena Bay. The islands were owned by various cooperative farming communities known as *ejidos* and a few well-connected politicians whose families were granted the land over a century ago as reward for their revolutionary loyalty.

Fish hoped to save it all from development: Baja beachfront, mangrove shoreline, miles of sand dunes, tidal flats and marled coast—every available stretch preserved forever in an unbreakable trust. He would give it a proper moniker so visitors knew its distinction.

Call it the Magdalena Bay Marine Sanctuary.

Safe haven for sea turtles, juvenile billfish, clams and shrimp, and every other warm-water exotic endangered by overfishing and water pollution.

Now, as he adjusted his tall frame on the back of the black-and-white mule and began his trot along the beach, he felt hopeful again. Especially after the only woman he'd felt a stirring for in years had to leave so abruptly. Toozie McGill, the most beautiful private investigator in the business. A fearless woman with a wit as sharp as a marlin spike. She'd come to Baja to find a missing client, walked into the wrong Cabo San Lucas nightclub, and ended up on a boat to nowhere with evil at the wheel. She'd survived, but not without exacting a deadly toll with a fish bat to the face of her abductor. Fish rescued her and hours later reunited her with her missing client. But then, on the way back to his island getaway for a long-overdue vacation, Toozie received a call from a frantic relative. Fish banked his seaplane and dropped her at Marina de La Paz for the short taxi ride to the airport—and a rain check on the vacation.

There was more to it, of course—a tangle of emotions that began with the teenage daughter he had to leave behind when the death threats became unmanageable. Charlotte had been a junior in high school, independent and strong-willed like her mother. Fish knew he couldn't expect her to flee south with him, not with the opportunities that awaited her. As valedictorian and captain of her high school lacrosse team, Charlotte had countless choices for college. Her love for Aunt Toozie was also limitless. And so it was agreed that Charlotte would stay behind, change her last name, and have no contact with her father, the billionaire pariah with a bull's-eye on his head—not until the zealots' hatred of him lost its fire. It would be a few years at most, he'd been certain.

But a few years had somehow turned to a decade, and he'd yet to see his daughter. At first, he'd been reluctant to call or send letters to either Charlotte or Toozie in case they were being watched. It was safer to remain distant. He felt certain they both knew this. But still it hurt. Finally, as she would've been entering her junior year of college, he couldn't bear it any longer. He reached out to her. Indirectly. Covertly.

And was rebuffed.

Fish forced away the ache in his heart. He tried not to think of his daughter's rejection of him, or her youthful eyes, or Toozie's easy laughter. Had she somehow bought into the tabloid treatment of him? Or was she afraid? Of that he couldn't blame her. He missed them both, and for different reasons, needed them back in his life. His daughter would be twenty-six, long out of college now. Working, for all he knew, and raising a family.

Just months ago, he'd been buttressing his courage for another attempt at contact when he'd received deadly evidence of his enemies' continuing thirst for revenge. Wrestler-turned-bodyguard Snake Hissken had recognized him after all these years. Recognized him and nearly killed him. Had nearly killed Toozie, too.

How could he reinsert himself into his daughter's life when so many fanatics had wanted him dead? Still wanted him dead.

But Toozie was now back in his life. At least peripherally. She was fearless and would help him make up for the lost years. He knew she was waiting for him to find a way to do the right thing. Letting him decide how and when to reenter Charlotte's life and try to rekindle her love for him. Waiting and watching like a seasoned private investigator—and slowly running out of patience. Of that he was sure.

She'd made it clear that Charlotte had read his caution, his wild fear for her safety, as aloofness. That was madness, of course. He would have given everything to be back with his daughter, but he had come to understand that the haters would always hate, and he could never risk the lives of those he loved, no matter how badly he missed them, no matter how it sullied his reputation.

Yet a balance had to be struck, and he must find a way to strike it. He had to make sure his daughter understood. He had to prove his love to her, face-to-face, with ten years' worth of hugs and heartfelt I love yous.

He swallowed wistfully and stared out at the wakening bay, returning his thoughts to what had kept him occupied these lonely years. Soon all of this coastline and the surrounding islands would be protected from the backhoes. And if he succeeded, it would be the perfect quinella to his recent assault on a fleet of illegal long-liners. Commercial trawlers plying the inshore waters like ravenous sharks. Without proper permits. Stinking of graft and marlin blood.

Fish had spotted them before they laid their first stringer of deadly hooks. He had reported the violation to his Mexican attorney in La Paz, the powerfully connected Armado Fox, who got nowhere with his complaints. So Fish went commando by way of a personal submarine ordered specifically for the task of snipping thousands of illegal fishing hooks from miles of monofilament fishing line. The titanium rotors had been like razor-edged helicopter blades putting an end to the undersea carnage. Boatloads of exotic game fish had been saved from slaughter. Millions of dollars in damaged fishing gear had sunk to the bottom. Long-liner captains demanded answers. Government officials promised inquiries. Pesky reporters inquired about a rumored underwater *chupacabra* roaming the trenches off Magdalena Bay, engulfing thousands of hooked fish, and tearing apart gear like tissue.

Tucking away his submarine deep in the mangroves near his sand-dune-island home, Fish took advantage of the hullabaloo and offered sea-monster specials and half-priced drinks at his beachfront bar. He also loaned his seaplane to environmentalists flying banners demanding an end to illegal long-lining, and he hosted a meeting of local *curanderas,* who applauded the resurrection of angry sea-gods.

Within days the long-liners moved out, the investigations ended, and the reporters returned to more dependably sensational crimes—border-town beheadings and mountains of Mexican *mota.*

And soon the game fish returned. In droves. Which in turn attracted the attention of marina developers and hoteliers interested in cashing in on the whims of the big-game angler. Fish welcomed them all to his bar, and while they sketched their forests of docks and bayside putting greens, the wealthy expatriate instructed his high-powered Mexican attorney to negotiate options on every stretch of sand within fifty miles. The worldwide recession, combined with prolific media coverage of Mexican drug cartels, kept the price more than affordable for a man of Fish's wealth. Add the tens of millions recently offered by the Nature Conservancy, and the purchase was a downright bargain.

The thought of his end run around the developers lifted Fish's broad shoulders as he sat astride his mule and stretched a smile across his face as they trotted up the beach. He was still smiling, absently twirling the braided tail of his sun-washed goatee, when explosive music shattered the dawn air just inland from them. Rasping metallic rock shook miniature avalanches from the surrounding sand dunes.

Fish heeled Mephistopheles in the flanks and galloped toward the sound. Moments later he slowed at the sight of a decrepit Winnebago parked in a clearing above a rolling sand dune less than a hundred yards from the shoreline, and just half a mile from Puerto San Carlos where Fish's bar, Cantina del Cielo, would soon open for breakfast.

As the morning sun breached the horizon and the last of the pargo-colored clouds spread across the sky, Fish cautiously approached the Winnebago, but he stopped when a lone cow trotted into view. It paused at the sight of the towering man atop the strange-looking mule, then bolted in terror when the screeching chorus of Twisted Sister again split the air.

Apparently, it, too, wasn't going to take it anymore.

Neither was Fish.

He often came across campers during his morning mule-back hunts for rare shells and unusual flotsam for display at his cantina. Most were the hardier form of sightseer in search of desolate terrain and unmolested beach. None, however, blasted Twisted Sister at dawn.

Thirty miles of corrugated dirt road through bleak desert and triple-digit heat substantially narrowed the guest list to vagabonds, nomads, and adventure seekers. Tourists in search of bays without Sea-Doos, shorelines without high-rises.

Ports without cruise ships.

The anti-Cabo crowd.

But more and more Fish was encountering scalawags with less sense than a geoduck. Witless college boys with stingray bloodlust. Bonehead Texans armed with birdshot. And now this broken-down Winnebago with its early-morning rock concert. The trend was alarming. Maybe it was the Internet that brought them—thrill-seekers lured by the vastness of land brimming with banditos and beheadings.

Fish had never heard of a beheading in southern Baja, and most banditos worked border towns and resort destinations— destinations Fish planned to strongly recommend to the current head-bangers and their traveling noise circus.

The handsome expatriate dismounted and retrieved an empty tequila bottle, carelessly tossed into the dune, half buried in the sand. After tucking it into one of the two saddlebags draped over Mephistopheles's haunches, he hopped back aboard the mule, loosened the tie-down on the machete sheathed to his thigh, and rode into the bedlam.

The rust bucket of a Winnebago had veered off-road and was stuck in a stretch of sandy loam. The side door hung askew, its latch a twisted metal hanger threaded through a ragged hole in the aluminum siding. Other holes along the shell of the oversized vehicle had been halfheartedly patched with drywall putty that sagged in the sun like bags of skin. No attempt had been made to paint over the globs of putty, which had darkened with engine exhaust and road dirt.

Rounding the Winnebago, Fish considered the balding tires, the missing side mirrors, the spiderwebbed windshield. One of the headlights was shattered, and the front grill had been spray-painted with the slogan *Road Slayer*. Off to the side was a portable card table placed recklessly close to a fire pit smoking with the remnants of plastic plates and blackened hot dogs. A forest of empty tequila bottles led Fish's sea-green eyes to a waist-high boulder with a speaker dock and an iPod upon it.

Fish rode to the boulder and silenced Dee Snider's scream. The sudden stillness exacerbated the ringing in his ears. He dismounted and caught the echo of a series of loud grunting sounds emanating from the opposite side of the sand dune. Fish vaulted onto the mule's back and rode toward the sound.

As he crested the dune, he saw three bare-chested men in skin-tight shorts dancing around an enormous cardón cactus.

"Left, right, left!" one of the men yelled, and all three began punching the trunk of the saguaro-like cactus.

"Switch!" another called out.

The men reversed direction.

"Kidney punch!"

All three crouched and threw vicious upper cuts. Green pulp exploded around their fists.

"Switch!"

"Front kick!"

"Spinning backhand!"

Fish yelled, "Rear-naked choke!"

The men stopped midpunch and gawked in disbelief at the barefoot man trotting toward them on a mule.

The largest of the three recovered first. "Who the fuck are you?" he demanded, taking an aggressive step toward Fish.

Fish unsheathed the machete. "You're about to kill that cactus."

"That's the idea," the man said, stopping to eye the machete. Fish saw the flash of a predator in the fighter's pupils. The man's head was shaved to display a bloodred tattoo of the letters UFC. Sweat drained down his heavy face.

"It's illegal to molest a cardón," Fish continued.

The three men looked at one another, then back to Fish.

"Who you calling a molester?" spat the oldest of the three, his face red, his nose veined with the telltale signs of a career drunk.

"He doesn't mean that kind of molestation, Jimbo," the third and youngest of the group said, wiping a gloved hand across his patchy blond beard.

Jimbo shrugged. "I don't care what kind he means. He can shove it up his ass."

"That cactus you're kicking the guts out of is a hundred years old," Fish explained. "Those new arms just above your heads? They take a century to get that size. The massive ones near the top probably sprouted about the time Cortez came sniffing around for gold."

"Who?" the big one asked.

"Cortez," the young fighter answered. "Spanish conquistador. Sailed to Mexico from Spain looking for gold."

"Shut the hell up, Mikey," ordered the first man. The grin he turned on Fish held no mirth, and it was missing several teeth as well. "Mikey thinks reading's important."

"He the one who scraped off the thorns?" Fish asked, glancing down at the wedge-shaped rocks near their feet, their sharp edges stained green with cactus hide.

"Listen, old-timer," the big one continued. "We've got nothing against you or your donkey, but we're not leaving until our opponent falls."

"She's a mule."

"Don't really matter."

Fish sighed and pushed for clarification. "Your 'opponent'?"

"As long as this cactus is still standing, we're still training."

"Training?"

"Ultimate Fighter competition. Tryouts are next month in El Centro."

Fish removed his mullet-skin cap and wiped his brow. He glanced at the rising sun, then reached for the metal crimp holding his chin braid. "This cactus isn't falling," he said. "If it's training you want, try jogging to the beach and swimming across the bay a few times." He replaced his cap. "And maybe lay off the tequila."

The big guy shrugged. "Beer's full of carbs." He turned his back on Fish and resumed his pounding on the pulped cactus flesh. "Break's over, boys!"

The other two joined in.

When Fish heeled Mephistopheles toward the cactus, the leader spun and raised his fists. "Put away the blade, old man, or I drop the mule *and* break your face."

Without pausing, Fish rode close, swung the machete, and sliced off the lowest-hanging cactus arm. The big man, despite his promise to deck the mule, had taken a step back at its approach and managed to locate himself directly under the plummeting branch. The cactus arm slammed into his head like a thorny sandbag and dropped him to the ground unconscious, tiny tributaries of blood seeping from his pincushioned scalp.

The other two fighters looked on in disbelief.

"Next?" Fish asked.

Neither man spoke. The man on the ground groaned.

"Cardón thorns are long and sharp," Fish explained, his tone casual, almost friendly. "That branch weighs at least a hundred pounds. He'll need a doctor to dig them out. If not, infection's going to set in. The quicker you break camp, the better."

"Tank's undefeated," the baby-faced man said in astonishment, turning to his red-faced comrade. "We better get him to the doc, Jimbo."

Jimbo ignored Mikey and stepped forward. "You're a fucking dead man," he growled.

Fish swung the machete again. This time the blade cleaved a smaller arm from the cactus. The fighter realized his mistake and tried to block the blow. The spine-covered branch pinned Jimbo's forearm to his chest and bounced him flat to the dirt. Oxygen fled his lungs like bats from a cave.

Mikey looked up at the remaining arms of the cactus, then looked at Fish. "I thought you wanted to save it."

"After the pummeling you three gave it, pruning's its only chance." He feigned another overhead swing and sent the young man sprinting back toward camp.

"There's a doctor in town," he called out after him. "Her name's Minerva."

As he watched the young man disappear over the sand dune, Fish heeled Mephistopheles toward the bay and took the shoreline back to Cantina del Cielo. The restaurant would open soon, and the bar's resident parrot, Chuy, would be wondering where he was, along with two hungover iguanas and a notorious mescal-maker named Skegs.

CHAPTER THREE

San Evaristo, Baja California Sur

Roscoe Ferrill and his newlywed wife, Tawny, launched their twelve-foot aluminum skiff from the beach in front of the village of San Evaristo and were soon trolling the shoreline for sierra mackerel. It was dawn, and the sea stretched like flatiron into a brush-fire sunrise. Both wore swimsuits and baseball caps, and matching polarized sunglasses. Tawny, who sat at the bow facing her young husband, held a lightweight fishing rod off the port gunwale. Roscoe stood at the stern, steering the outboard engine with one hand and holding his own light fishing rod with the other. His lure paralleled the starboard side of the skiff and was set at a staggered distance from the other lure to avoid tangle.

"Sailor's warning," Roscoe commented as he checked the drag on the small Shimano reel.

"No way," Tawny said, her long brown hair held back by a faded orange bandanna. "I can see for miles." She set the rod to her lap and slipped into a sweatshirt to block the draft created by the moving boat.

"Red sky at night, sailor's delight. Red sky in the morning—"

"Hookup!" Tawny hollered, and leaned against the weight of the doubled-over rod in her hands.

The fish plummeted for the seafloor, then rocketed for the surface and leaped, banking its fins off the sunlight and sending a rooster tail of water across the early-morning chop. Rod tip high, Tawny turned the fish and slowly worked it to the boat.

"Nice fish," Roscoe remarked as he netted the log-sized sierra.

The line was reset, and for the next hour the newlyweds crisscrossed the channel between Isla San Jose and the peninsula, catching two more sierras and a pompano. At the midpoint of the island, Tawny motioned toward a short stretch of beach.

"Beachcombing break?" she asked, shucking her sweatshirt. She removed her sunglasses and blinked away a line of sweat from her almond-colored eyes.

Roscoe gave her a thumbs-up and veered into the shallows.

"Jesus," he said after killing the engine and coasting up the sand wedging the bow like an anchor. He stepped to the beach and ran his hands through his spongy head of black curls. "Those look like fresh rock slides."

"Quake," Tawny said as she scanned the rubble. "Radio said the fault line was fifty miles north of La Paz. Along the seafloor. That's around this island somewhere. Luckily nobody lives out here."

"Somebody's been here recently, though," he said, pointing at the footprints crowding the sand. "Probably picked the beach clean."

"Bummer," she said. Hopping to the sand, she stepped free of her bikini bottoms. "Plan B." She removed her top and tossed it and her sunglasses to Roscoe before racing into the water. "You're it!" She swam toward the bend of the island and disappeared around the rocks.

Roscoe dropped her things and tore off his board shorts, tripping before his feet were free. He scrambled up, blowing away sand from his whiskered lips, and raced into the water after her. When he caught up, she was scrambling up a rocky outcropping toward a plastic yellow bag caught on a barnacle.

"Can you believe it?" she called back to him, pulling it free. "Plastic bag way out here." She tried to crumple it in her hand, then scowled at it. "Loaded with trash, too. People just tossing ugliness in all this beauty."

"You're beautiful," he said. "You balance it out."

Grinning, she rolled her eyes at him, then straightened up and frowned. "Uh-oh," she said, pointing over his head. "We gotta go, honey."

Roscoe turned and saw the whitecaps skittering across the channel. "That's nothing," he said, turning back to her. "We've got time." He swam up to the rock with a salacious glint to his eyes.

Tawny offered a teasing pose from her rocky stage. "Wasn't it you who mentioned sailor's warning?"

"Yeah, but—"

"Sorry, cowboy." She wrapped the open end of the plastic bag tight around her palm and dived with it over his head.

By the time Roscoe caught up, she was already clothed in her bathing suit and working the skiff into the water.

"You weren't kidding," he said, reluctantly pulling on his shorts. He shook the salt water from his head of curly hair.

"Help me launch. Wind's picking up."

Moments later they were zooming across the channel, salt water spraying into a stiffening wind. By the time they made San Evaristo, both were white-knuckled and flushed. Behind them the sea swarmed as if covered in waterborne locusts. Sand whipped across the shoreline and stung their ankles. Their camp had been reduced to a pile of collapsed beach chairs, an upended beach umbrella, and a tent splayed awkwardly against the door of their '72 Land Cruiser.

"Time to pack," Tawny said.

"And go where?"

"Pacific side."

He nodded. "Mag Bay's a straight shot across. Five hours max. I've been reading about a funky palapa bar run by an expat."

"Bar sounds good."

"Miles of mangroves."

"Mangroves." Her eyes lit up. "Big fish like to hide in mangroves."

"Not just any fish. Black snook. Nearly impossible to hook, the book says."

"For mortals, maybe." Tawny flexed her biceps.

Roscoe pulled her into an embrace. "I wouldn't mind a cheap motel and a shower."

"They probably have one of those there, too."

A grin split Roscoe's face. "You ice the fish. I'll load the outboard."

CHAPTER FOUR

La Paz, Baja California Sur

Manolín sat at the plastic table across from his grandfather and finished his ice cream. *Fresa con caramelo.* He wanted to make it last, but the corner fan in the small *paletería* was no match for the midday heat. He engulfed the melting treat, then raised his head and stared through the shop window, across the famous *malecón,* where the boats lazed against their anchor chains in the calm bay.

"They will be here soon, *Abuelo.*"

Zaragosa nodded. He'd spent a week in the hospital after his fellow *pangeros* found him clinging to the cliffside boulder, dehydrated, his arm crooked and badly swollen. He was alive, but heartbroken.

As his village's most experienced *pangero,* he was known for his shrewdness at sea. He rarely missed a day of fishing and always returned safely. He worked alone, without a radio or life vest or any other expensive navigational or safety equipment. He relied on intuition and experience and courage. But the discovery of the pearl had changed him. He'd been so focused on the magnificence of the discovery that he hardly remembered swimming for the oysters. How he'd missed the roiling sea and the darkening sky was a mystery to him. Surely it wasn't greed that had numbed his senses. He'd never pursued wealth. Never cared for the complications of too many pesos. He was content living day to day at the mercy of the sea—a sea that had treated him well over the decades.

No, he'd been blinded by the opportunity the pearls had represented for the boy, and the old fisherman felt his heart sink at the loss of the opportunity to provide it. A chance that proved so fleeting, it appeared cruel in hindsight. Circumstances caused by the tormented ghost of Mechudo, for no God was that malevolent. The find's suddenness had clouded his reason. Rather than heed the warnings, he'd dreamed of a house with a solid door and glass windows, a proper education for the boy, new clothes and comfortable shoes. It was a fancy only a fool would entertain— such nonsense rightfully dashed by the dead boy's spirit, whipping up a *chubasco* and then the terrible tremors of the seafloor.

"What is it?" Manolín asked, having noticed his grandfather's distant eyes.

Zaragosa drew a long breath and blinked ruefully. He shrugged, and his heavily cast arm jarred the flimsy table.

Manolín leaned forward. "You have not spoken since we sat down. Are you angry with me?"

Zaragosa's eyes clouded, and he brushed his free hand at his bearded face, the white hairs dramatic against the deep brown skin of his fingers. "My thoughts are back at the island, *Nieto*." He reached out and patted the boy's head kindly. "I am glad to have this moment. I promised you, remember?"

"I thought you were gone." Manolín looked away, and then added quietly, "Forever."

"Yes," Zaragosa said. "I am sorry." A sudden thought crinkled the skin at the corners of his eyes. He motioned for Manolín to move closer, and then whispered, "I have a secret to tell you."

"A secret?" Manolín asked excitedly.

"You must promise to tell no one."

"I swear."

Zaragosa glanced furtively around the empty shop. "I discovered a famous bed of pearl oysters."

The boy's eyes widened.

"That is why I stayed at sea too long. I lost my senses and tried to bring too many pearls home." He felt his heart race and he paused. "The storm took me by surprise."

"How many pearls did you find?"

"Only three, but they were of rare color, and one was fat and heavy. As big as a pitahaya and almost as colorful."

The boy looked away again.

"What is it, Manolín?"

"I don't want you to go back there."

"But a few more pearls like that can buy us a bigger boat and a house with thick walls and running water."

"Please, *Abuelo*. The sea is angry with you."

The old man shook his head. "It was not the sea. It was this foolish old man. I was reckless. I should have immediately taken the first pearl to the church, to honor our village and to make amends for the death of Mechudo. I should have stopped and come back for you. Presented the pearl to the priest before returning for more." He closed his eyes and composed his thoughts. He opened them and found the boy's gaze. "I was greedy, *niño*. But I will be more cautious next time." He glanced around the empty shop for the second time and said with a conspiratorial tone, "And I will take you with me."

The boy's eyes lit up.

"You have strong lungs and you swim like a *pargo*."

Manolín beamed at the compliment. "But we lost our boat. How can we collect the oysters without a boat?"

Zaragosa winked. "An old fisherman has many tricks, *Nieto*."

CHAPTER FIVE

Puerto San Carlos, Baja California Sur

After his confrontation with the wannabe UFC fighters, Fish returned to the small port town of San Carlos. He followed the pebbly shoreline to his shuttered eatery, Cantina del Cielo, and trotted Mephistopheles to her paddock with its mini-palapa built beside a cluster of spindly armed mesquite trees at the edge of Magdalena Bay. The sun had fully risen and was skipping coins of light across the bay. Pelicans taking advantage of the sharp glare crashed beak-first into schools of unsuspecting sardines rising with the breaking day.

Fish tied the mule to the post hook, and then uncoiled the hose kept beside the restaurant and added fresh water to the hollowed-out date palm that formed the trough. He dumped oats into an adjacent bin and then brushed the dust from Mephistopheles's mottled coat. As he worked, he could hear Chuy, the scarlet macaw, singing out bawdy drink orders from high in the rafters of the open-air Cantina del Cielo. *Tequila con sangrita* quickly followed by a guttural *chingoso* seemed to be the flavor of the day. Fish had started toward the bar when the sound of a souped-up car engine split the quietude.

Half expecting to see the cacti assailants, Fish did a double take at the sight of a neon-green Volkswagen Bug speeding into the empty parking lot. Its top had been sheared off and replaced with a heavy-duty roll bar. The car skidded to a stop on oversized knobby tires, and through the fresh plume of dust Fish saw a series of cartoon worms painted across the hood.

Mescal worms. Smiling, red-eyed, annelids with the words *Macho Mescal* forming halos above wrinkled foreheads.

Skegs.

A tall, dark-skinned man with ringlets of kelp-colored hair and blue jay eyes stepped from the car. "Man, I hope Mamacita's fired up the flatiron," Skegs said, waving his hand in front of his face to clear the air. "I'm famished."

"'Macho Mescal'?"

"New company name. You like it?"

"Has a certain ring to it." Lightly fingering the braid beneath his tackle-box chin, Fish tilted his head to get a better look at the artwork on the passenger door. "Angelic earthworms, though, might take some getting used to."

"Come on, man. You named a drinking establishment Heaven's Bar. Can't get more sacrilegious than that."

Fish grinned. "But a kit car? Doesn't sound like the Skegs I know."

"You mean, my butt-kicking Baja One Thousand mobile? Got to expose the new brand, baby. What better way than at the world's baddest off-road race?"

"You're entering the Baja One Thousand?" Fish asked incredulously.

"*We're* entering it," Skegs said, his smile sparkling in the morning sun.

Fish coughed out a short laugh and headed for the cantina's front door, reaching into the pocket of his sailcloth pants for the key.

Skegs jogged up to his friend. "It'll be awesome, man. I'll even let you drive some. When we need to go slow. So I can wave to my fans. Give them time to check out the graphics."

Ignoring him, Fish unlocked the door and began walking the perimeter of the bar, unhinging the dozens of windows that helped block the afternoon wind while allowing an unobstructed view of the water.

Skegs followed closely behind, latching the windows to the overhead lintels. "What say you, wingman?" he asked when they'd finished.

"Maybe."

"Yes!" Skegs pumped his fist. "You're going to love it, man."

"I said maybe."

"Which is more than halfway to yes."

Fish shook his head wearily. Through the open windows he could smell the brine of the bay waft in with the coppery overtones of the nearby mangroves with their thick mud and clams and bay shrimp. He walked to the corner jukebox and punched in classic John Prine.

Free songs for customers night and day.

Everything from Joe Purdy to Pepe Aguilar.

And Prine. Lots of Prine.

As an angel from Montgomery soared across the room, Chuy released a piercing squawk and dropped from the rafters. He circled once, then exited through an open window to join a flock of seagulls wheeling above a bottlenose dolphin crashing the surface and feeding with the pelicans.

"Smart bird," Skegs commented as he ducked behind the circular bar that wrapped the center beam of the palapa like the crow's nest of an ancient ship, and poured himself an icy mug of Tecate. "This song could depress a monk." He took a deep slug and set the glass to the planked bar top, refurbished from a wrecked schooner.

The cowbell on the front door jangled, and a stooped woman entered the bar.

"*Buenas días,*" Fish said reverently as the old woman shuffled across the hard-packed sand of the outer area.

Mamacita Espinoza nodded with a gummy smile. As the eighty-year-old cook passed, she swept up the sweating mug of Tecate from the bar, downed it in a single gulp, belched, then continued into the back kitchen and began prepping breakfast.

Peering after her, Skegs said, "That's got to be the oldest succubus on the planet."

"Who single-handedly tripled our business last year. That is one valuable woman."

"Man, you keep talking like that, you're gonna catch the curse."

"No such thing."

"Six dead husbands is definitely a curse."

"Not a problem." Fish gave him a wry smile. "Unless you're planning to marry her."

Skegs shuddered at the thought. He plucked a clean mug from the drying rack and poured a fresh beer. "She does make a killer plate of huevos rancheros, I admit."

"Which is on the house today," Fish said, then strolled to the solar-powered refrigerator behind the bar and removed a jug of mango juice. "I might need your help later."

"Sierras are schooling," Skegs said excitedly. "And, having fished with you, I know you're going to need some pointers." He exaggerated a glance at his waterproof dive watch and added, "Luckily, I happen to have the day free."

Ignoring his theatrics, Fish halved a lime and squeezed it into a glass of crushed ice, then followed it with the mango juice. "I ran into some bozos this morning beating a cardón to death with their bare fists."

Skegs nearly choked on his swallow of beer. "Beating a cactus barehanded? Had to be white guys. No Mexican's that dumb."

Fish agreed with a grunt as he drank his juice.

"How many bozos?"

"Three. Traveling in a beat-up Winnebago. Buff young guys. They mentioned training for the UFC."

"You took on three UFC dudes?"

"It wasn't much of a fight."

Skegs eyed him over the rim of the beer mug.

"Mephistopheles helped a little."

"Jesus, man. You trampled them with a mule?"

"Dropped the first two with a couple of cactus arms. The third one ran off."

Skegs brushed a weedy bang from his baby blues and whistled.

Fish continued. "They should be with the doc by now. I expect they'll stop in afterward looking for payback."

"They know you own this place?"

"It's a small town."

Skegs nodded, then nodded again. "I get it. Man, I'm touched. You need a warrior to protect you."

"More like a workhorse. After breakfast we'll hop over to the island and load the shark cage."

Skegs nearly choked on his beer for the second time. "You're going to feed these guys to the sharks?"

Fish was about to answer, when Mamacita crossed the bar with two plates of huevos rancheros: steaming refried beans topped with shredded cabbage and minced cilantro, two fried eggs, and a hefty dose of crumbled goat cheese, all of it swimming in a moat of homemade green salsa.

Mamacita set the plates to the bar top and winked at Skegs, who flinched as if he'd been slapped.

"Salud," she said.

As she turned to go, a pair of stiff-legged iguanas surfaced suddenly from a nearby bar stool. They climbed to the bar top and ambled toward the food. Mamacita reached into her apron and slid a rotting plantain down the bar. Pancho and Lefty pounced.

As Skegs watched the lizards devour the banana, Mamacita scooped his fresh beer into her wrinkled hand and returned to the kitchen.

"I told you, man," Skegs said as he started in on his breakfast. "Black magic. That woman could steal a broom from a witch."

"I think she likes you."

Skegs's eyes flamed like an acetylene torch.

"You could be lucky number seven," Fish added.

"I'm starting to not like you."

"At least you'd eat well," Fish deadpanned. "Unless the curse is in the food."

CHAPTER SIX

Puerto San Carlos, Baja California Sur

By the time Roscoe and Tawny rolled into Puerto San Carlos, it was early afternoon. The wind had weakened, and as they drove though the tiny town with its colorful shotgun shacks and solo motel, only a light Pacific breeze ruffled the bay.

"I'm starving," Tawny said, looking up from her tattered Baja guidebook. "Cantina del Cielo gets a five-clam rating from the Baja Bhagwan. Best sand dab tostadas in the world, she says."

"Baja Bhagwan?"

"The traveling Zen lady of Baja Sur. Martina something or other. Used to publish an expat newspaper. Now she travels around looking for all things cool south of the border."

"Never heard of her."

"That's why you have me, honey."

Roscoe shot her an inquisitive look.

"She also claims that this Cantina del Cielo has the coldest beer in Baja, guaranteed."

"A beer-drinking Bhagwan. Love it!"

Minutes later the old Land Rover pulled into the clamshell lot and parked beside a rusted-out Winnebago with missing side mirrors and a cracked windshield. Half a dozen pickups, two Jeeps, and a souped-up neon-green Volkswagen Bug with its top sheared off populated one side of the lot. The other side held a cluster of off-road motorcycles, and a vintage Ford Woody stacked high with surfboards. At the far corner of the lot were a tight grove of mesquite trees and a black-and-white mule standing beneath a palapa. And beyond that, a small pier extended toward a far-off sailboat with a crooked mast, a few yachts, and a seaplane. A refurbished trawler with a shark cage on its back deck was sidling up to the end of the pier.

"Man, I already dig this place," Roscoe said.

"Looks like the Bhagwan knows her stuff," Tawny agreed, and quickly changed in her seat into a pair of board shorts and a lightweight cotton pullover. She stepped from the Land Rover, adjusted the Leatherman fishing tool strapped to her belt, and looked out at the trawler, which a tall, dark-skinned deckhand was securing to the dock. Above the deckhand was a forest of fishing rods framing the upper deck behind the helm, along with two kayaks and a handsome, broad-shouldered captain with an oddly shaped cap and a braided goatee. He was staring out at the parking lot, his square jaw set, his eyes focused on the Winnebago.

"Bet those guys know where we can find a black snook," Roscoe said.

"First we try out those sand dab tostadas." Tawny was turning to kiss him, when a commotion at the Winnebago caught her attention.

A man with a bandaged head had flung open the broken side door and stumbled into the sunlight, waving a baseball bat. As she and Roscoe watched, he marched toward the trawler and bellowed out a demand that the captain meet him like a man. Close behind came a second drunk, his arm in a homemade sling, his other arm raised above his head in a fist. They both spewed profanities as they approached the small dock. A third man, baby-faced with a patchy beard, hung back at the open door and shouted for his friends to come back.

"Should we do something?" Tawny asked.

"I have a feeling the fishermen have it covered."

As the drunks hit the pier, the deckhand reached over the gunwale and hefted a good-sized nylon cast net out onto the planks. He draped the weighted end over his shoulder, took a few steps forward, then stopped and widened his stance. He brushed thick weedy bangs from his wraparound sunglasses and grinned.

"Out of the way, Tonto!" the lead aggressor slurred loudly as he continued to advance.

The second man followed suit. "Ain't no Injun with a nest of strings gonna stop the future of the UFC!"

"Strike one," Skegs said, casually adjusting the weighted net.

The big man slowed and the second man with the bad arm collided into him. "Sorry, Tank," he said, then straightened and urged his pal forward. "Come on, man! Knock this asshole's head off. Lone Ranger up on that boat needs an ass whooping."

Skegs's sharklike grin grew. "Strike two."

Tank cocked the bat at him, peeling back his lips to expose his missing tooth. "So, what's your plan? Them little lead weights ain't worth shit."

In a single swift, whirling motion, Skegs pitched the net. It unfurled over the two like an enormous umbrella, and they gaped stupidly at it as it settled directly over them. When the skirt of leaded weights clattered to the dock in a perfect circle around them, Skegs hauled back on the cinch cord, closing the trap at their feet. Both men tripped and fell hard to the planking. Fish appeared at the gunwale of the trawler, leaned his upper body over it, and helped haul the bellowing, thrashing human catch aboard and into the shark cage. Skegs yanked the net free of them, and Fish slammed the door and latched the bars with a stainless steel padlock.

"Nice toss," Fish said.

"Anytime, Captain." Skegs rewrapped the net and pitched it down the deck toward the starboard corner of the stern. Then he retrieved a beer from his personal cooler and looked back at the baby-faced man hiding in the mesquite trees. "Fun's over," he called out. "Want a beer?"

Before Baby-Face could answer, the one named Tank jumped to his feet and rattled his cage, his unraveled head bandage revealing a whiskered skull pocked with raging red bumps pulsing with infection. "Let us out of here, goddammit!" he demanded, shaking the bars of the cage like an enraged orangutan.

"First things first," Fish said.

"This is bullshit!" the other man yelled, slowly climbing to his feet and cradling his bad arm.

"Seems we've got a conundrum," Skegs said, sipping his beer. "What to do with two mangy dogs caged for their own safety."

Tank gave the cage another shake, this one so violent his buddy almost lost his feet again.

Fish shook his head disapprovingly. "Please don't do that."

"Fuck you!"

Fish glanced above the cage and eyed the cable running to the power wench. He nodded to Skegs, who engaged the motor. The cage lifted from the deck and swayed with the shifting weight of its inhabitants.

"We have probably a dozen witnesses, peering out the windows all around," Fish said to Tank. "They'll be only too glad to tell the authorities what you're up to."

"Authorities?" Tank spat. "What fucking authorities? This is Mexico, you idiot."

Fish gave a hand signal, and Skegs maneuvered the cage above the boat's gunwale and expertly set it into the water up to the men's knees.

"Hey, you can't do this!" the second man shouted.

"He's bluffing," Tank said. He stared hard at Fish, his face red, a fresh webbing of blood trickling from his pincushioned head. He brushed it away from his bloodshot eyes and sneered at him. "You've got five seconds to let us go before Mikey torches your bar." He pointed confidently toward the cantina.

Fish turned and saw Babyface kneeling at the entrance to the bar with a can of gasoline and a lighter.

Tank started counting down from five.

"Come on, guys, please let them go," Mikey implored Fish and Skegs, his face ashen. "I'll make them leave. I promise. I don't want to do this!"

Fish started to motion for Skegs to bring the cage aboard, when a blur of scaly green flew through the bar's open door and landed on the baby-faced man's head and chest. He screamed and dropped the gas can, tripping as he fell backward, one iguana latched tightly to his face, the other to the front of his T-shirt.

Mamacita Espinoza stepped triumphantly through the door, scooped the gasoline from the ground, and reentered the bar with it.

"Don't be a pussy, Mikey!" Tank hollered. "Get off the ground and kick the shit out of that old bag of—"

Tank's last words were drowned out by the seawater. Skegs counted to thirty and brought the cage back to the surface.

Tank gulped at the air like a carp before beginning another barrage of insults. The cage lowered for a second time.

Back at the bar entrance, Mikey had escaped the claws of Pancho and Lefty, who were scurrying back to the bar. He stood wide-eyed and panting, blood beginning to stain his patchy blond beard.

"We tap!" Mikey called out. "Bring 'em up. We're going home. I swear. Gideon Bible." He dropped to his knees and cupped his hands in prayer.

Fish motioned to Skegs, who brought the cage to the surface. Both men were bug-eyed and scrimshaw white. Tank's bandages had fully loosened from his head and now stuck to his chest like a wet paper towel. The second man had also lost his homemade sling and was shivering uncontrollably.

"We can do this all day," Fish said. "But your buddy here wants to go home. We're okay with that, too." He turned to Mikey. "You or your buddies here ever return and we make sure the next cage they see is guarded with guns."

Tank slumped to the bottom of the cage.

Fish turned to Skegs. "If you'd be so kind as to direct them to the main road out of town." Hopping over the trawler's gunwale to the pier, he glanced at Roscoe and Tawny, who stood mesmerized by the ordeal. "Looks like I've got a couple of newcomers that could use an explanation."

Fish crossed the parking lot, tipping his cap to Mikey as he passed the Winnebago. Then he padded on bare feet to the couple standing beside an old Land Rover.

"Welcome to Cantina del Cielo," he said, and reached out his hand. "First round's on me."

CHAPTER SEVEN

La Paz, Baja California Sur

Zaragosa and Manolín watched through the ice cream shop as the *pangeros* from their village ambled up the boardwalk. The men had arrived by super *panga* after a day of fishing to ferry them back across the bay to their village of Evaristo thirty miles away. All four *pangeros* still wore their bloodstained yellow overalls and rubber boots, and their faces were salty from the long ocean trip. Zaragosa told Manolín to wait and exited the *paletería*. Minutes later he returned alone.

"*Listo?*" he asked his grandson.

"You sent them away?"

"They have only one boat."

"But—"

"Come." Zaragosa reached out and took Manolín by the hand. "It is a short walk."

Manolín followed his grandfather into the afternoon heat, both of them squinting in the harsh sunlight. The bay glimmered and rolled gently under the breeze the way a shawl flows down the shoulders of a señorita, the silky water turquoise in the shallows, deep emerald where the channels dropped deeper. Pelicans peppered the surface, emerging with their beaks pointed skyward, their gullets vibrating with sardines. Dozens of sailboats listed with the outgoing tide.

Zaragosa followed the boardwalk, limping from the soreness of the thorns removed from his heels, his new pair of huarache sandals hardly cushioning the wounds. They walked along the bay for three blocks until it ended at a forked roadway. Zaragosa took the bayside road, and minutes later stopped at the entrance to Marina de La Paz. The small marina was one of the oldest in La Paz with its hectare of docks that held a few hundred boats of varying lengths. They were mostly gringo-owned vessels, the majority sailboats and a smattering of small cruisers. A few large yachts populated the end caps where the water was deepest and the traffic lighter. The parking lot where Zaragosa and Manolín stood held only a small restaurant, a few trinket shops, and a mechanic's shop. It was the mechanic's shop that Zaragosa eyed thoughtfully.

"What is it, *Papi*?"

"The *mecánico* is an old friend."

"Then he will be happy to see you."

"It has been a very long time."

Manolín frowned. "Do you think he has forgotten you?"

Zaragosa wagged his head with a tired sigh. "We were just children. Once a month my father and the other men would come into town for supplies. If we were lucky, I and a few other children got to leave the village with the men for the day. They let us stay behind at the shore while they bought new nets and engine parts."

"Stay behind and do what?"

"Play. This was mostly beach back then. No boardwalk. Only this marina, smaller of course. We'd watched the rich *compañeros* park their expensive cars and stroll down to the water in their fancy clothes." He paused. "And we'd also look for trouble."

"What kind of trouble?"

"Kid trouble. Rock throwing. Sneaking onto boats that weren't ours." Zaragosa's voice took on a low tremor. "And one day, fight with the local boys."

"You and the *mecánico*?"

Zaragosa shook his head. "One of our village boys fought with him. *El Gordo* we called him. But he was more muscle that fat. And he was winning the fight. Had Carlos on the ground, and

Carlos wouldn't give up. *El Gordo* was angry. His fists were bloody and he had a look in his eyes that scared me. The other local boys were scared, too. They ran for help. But Carlos needed help right then. Before something terrible happened."

"And you saved him."

"*Sí,*" Zaragosa said in a whisper. "*El Gordo* was killing him. Punching him again and again. Carlos was unconscious and *El Gordo* wouldn't stop. I picked up a plank of wood that had washed ashore and then all I can remember was that ambulance taking both of them away." Zaragosa looked away. "Only one boy returned from the hospital."

Manolín released a small gasp. "*El Gordo* died?"

"I killed him to save a local boy I didn't even know."

"But you didn't mean to kill him, *Papi*. It was an accident." Manolín hugged his grandfather.

"Yes. But death is a heavy burden, *Nieto*. I was never allowed to return to La Paz. Not for years. Not until after my father had passed on. And by then Carlos was a grown man with a family. I did not want to bother him with the past."

"You have never seen him since that day?"

Zaragosa shook his head sadly.

"But you saved his life. He will be happy to thank you."

"I'd rather he lend us a *panga*." Zaragosa took a deep breath and started toward the mechanic's shop.

CHAPTER EIGHT

Puerto San Carlos, Baja California Sur

Roscoe and Tawny followed Fish into the crowded bar and joined him at a back table made from the wreckage of a wooden ship's hull that had washed ashore up the coast at Malarrimo. The refurbished hull was supported by driftwood legs planed and screwed into place by stainless steel screws. At the center of the table were a halved coconut shell filled with roasted peanuts, and a handful of paperback books held together by a pair of sand dollars secured with fishing weights and varnished as bookends.

Roscoe freed a bright yellow novel with a beer-stained caricature of a yellowfin tuna smoking a hand-rolled cigarette on the cover. He was about to ask if Fish had read the book, when the waitress appeared with two icy Carta Blancas and a frosty glass of soda.

"Welcome to Cantina del Cielo," Fish toasted, and took a pull of the Fresca.

Roscoe and Tawny were drinking from their beers when a scarlet macaw flew through an open window and landed on Fish's shoulder with a deafening squawk.

"Say hello to Chuy," Fish said.

"You let your parrot fly free?" Roscoe asked.

"He's a rescue parrot. Found him as a baby. When he was old enough to fly, we let him go. Seems he's fond of our peanuts."

Chuy hopped to the table and plucked a peanut from the coconut shell. He freed the inner seeds, flapped his wings, and soared to the rafters of the palapa.

"So about those snook," Tawny said, and reached down to lift their tackle box from the sand-packed floor. She set it to the table and opened the lid to an array of brightly colored lures and hooks and lead weights. "Our gear is mostly offshore stuff."

"Skegs's going to like the colors," Fish commented as he sifted through the miasma of gear.

"Who?" Roscoe asked.

Fish looked over at the young man. "My friend who threw the cast net over those yahoos. He's got the local knowledge, and he swears that the color of a lure makes a difference. He matches everything down to the swivel. Ties the perfect knot. Always uses new line. Over the top, to tell you the truth."

"But he knows how to catch the snook, right?" Tawny was excited. "Maybe he can guide us."

"He knows how *not* to catch them."

"Oh," she said, deflated.

"But he knows where they are."

Tawny's face brightened.

Fish reached into the bottom of the tackle box and removed a wadded-up yellow plastic bag with a questioning frown.

"Just some trash I picked up," Tawny said, watching Fish untangle the bag. "It was snagged on the rocks at San Jose."

"The island?" Fish asked. He turned the bag upside down and watched the crumpled ball of tinfoil bounce heavily to the tabletop. He lifted the ball of foil and peeled open the edges.

Tawny gasped.

"Are those pearls?" Roscoe asked, and snatched the largest gem from the grouping of three.

"They can't be," Tawny said, staring with a look of wonder at the orb in Roscoe's hand. "Pearls are small and white and round. That one's not small or even close to round."

"Or white." Roscoe's lips parted as he twirled the plum-colored specimen in the afternoon light. "Purple and red pearls. Are there such things?"

"May I?" Fish asked Roscoe, handing Tawny the two smaller spheres and reaching for the big pearl with its crooked edges.

Reluctantly, Roscoe dropped the horseshoe-crab-sized object into Fish's palm. The expatriate held it up in a shaft of sunlight. "I've never seen anything like it. Look at the way it pulses in the sunlight."

"As if it's filled with blood," Tawny said, an air of reverence in her voice.

"These can't be real," Roscoe said.

Tawny set the two smaller pearls on the table. "Why, because they're in a piece of tinfoil in some old plastic bag?"

"Exactly."

Fish lowered the large, off-shaped pearl, though kept it in his palm. "They'd be there if whoever found them hadn't planned on finding them."

"Huh?" Roscoe asked, his eyes unable to break free from the fiery pearl in Fish's hand.

"This had to be an unexpected find," Fish speculated. "Roscoe's right. No one heading out specifically for pearls would keep them in tinfoil and a plastic bag. Whoever found them wasn't looking for them."

"You think it was some random scuba diver?" Tawny asked.

He nodded. "I think it was a *pangero* surprised by the find."

The couple stared at him.

"Local fisherman," Fish explained. "The plastic bag is the kind they use at the local *tiendas*. Thin and cheap, not the thicker kind you get at the big grocery stores or the Wal-Mart in La Paz. And the color hasn't been washed out by the sun yet, which means it wasn't out there for very long. Maybe a week or so at the most."

"You think a local fisherman found these out at the island?" Roscoe asked.

Fish nodded. "The tinfoil's the other clue," he continued. "Every *pangero* I know takes a lunch with him. Usually rolled tacos or *machaca* burritos. I think he stumbled across an oyster bed and lucked into some pearls. The tinfoil and bag were his best bet for keeping them hidden and getting them back home safely."

"But he lost them," Tawny said. The smaller pearls had made their way back into her palm. "That's the part that doesn't make sense."

"Two weeks ago there was an earthquake centered near La Paz not far from Isla San Jose. The *pangero* could've capsized in the wave set off by the quake, lost the bag." Fish gently bounced the large teardrop pearl in his palm and paused in his thoughts, then squeezed his hand around the rare find and said, "That area was once famed for its oyster beds. A long time ago. Before the conquistadores got to them. And then the disease."

"Didn't Hemingway write about a Mexican pearl?" Roscoe wondered aloud.

"Steinbeck," Fish corrected him. "Based loosely on the famed oyster beds in the southern Sea of Cortez."

"So these could be real?" Tawny asked, rolling the pearls in her hand.

Fish sipped his Fresca. "I'd be willing to bet on it."

His guests exchanged a glance.

"But to be sure, I'd like to have them tested," Fish added, and extended his hand, palm up, to Tawny, who dropped the other two pearls into it alongside the big one.

"Um," Roscoe hesitated.

Fish said, "Here, keep one for good luck." He handed Roscoe one of the two smaller pearls. "You'll get the other two back soon, I promise. And just to guarantee it, I'll give you a cash deposit. Say five grand?"

Roscoe's brow hitched high with surprise, and he curled a forefinger at the remaining pearls. "Maybe for the big one. But I'll keep the other two just in case."

Fish handed back the other small pearl. "If they're real and from around here, we might be able to stop the harvest before it's too late."

"Too late for what?" Tawny asked.

"A sad repeat of history. The last time pearls like this were found, bad things happened. And not just to the oysters. There's a local legend about a young pearl diver who refused to give his first pearl to the church after he and a group of other divers had discovered a great pearl bed somewhere within a one- or two-day boat ride from La Paz."

"Isla San Jose is easily within that range," Tawny observed.

Fish nodded. "And when this particular young man found the first pearl oyster of the day, he was so excited by its size that he announced he would keep the prize for himself. But back then there was no scuba gear, and when the skin diver did not reappear, a few of his friends went down looking for him. They, too, failed to surface. Finally, the last members of the group poked their heads underwater, afraid to dive down, and saw the selfish young diver's arm clamped in the jaws of a giant oyster, his long black hair flowing with the current. The others had been washed away, never to be seen again."

"That's a terrible story," Tawny said.

"Yes. And very old. Recently I've heard rumors about infant oyster beds, but never proof of any pearls. If word gets out that the pearls are back, the oysters have no chance."

Roscoe shuddered. "Nor the locals, if the legend is true."

"Test the pearl," Tawny said, finishing her beer. "If it's local, we want to help. In the meantime, Roscoe and I'd like to get into one of those black snooks mentioned in the guidebook."

"Great," Fish said, dropping the large pearl into the breast pocket of his light green Guayabera shirt. "Skegs should be back any minute."

Roscoe straightened in his chair. "You said that guy *can't* fish worth a damn."

"He can't. But he'll get you on them. Then it's up to you." Fish stood and turned to leave. "Order anything you like. It's on the house."

"About that cash deposit you mentioned," Roscoe said.

Fish turned. "I'll let my bartender know. She'll get it for you before you leave."

"Thank you," Tawny said.

Fish tipped his hat and padded on bare feet across the sand-packed floor, unaware of the pale-faced man at a nearby table who busied himself with an unshucked peanut.

The stranger took a furtive glance at the tall barefoot man before motioning for the waitress. He needed to walk the town. Formulate a plan. And whatever plan he formulated would almost certainly involve those three men who'd been run off earlier by this man and his local Indian friend. Three muscle-heads with a grudge probably formulating their booze-infused revenge on the outskirts of town.

They'd be easy to convince to put together a world-class diversion while the stranger separated the big pearl from the powerful man with the braided goatee. The other two pearls were nothing special, hardly worth the effort of stealing. But the big one was spectacular, surely worth a small fortune—an easy and enticing payday for a cat burglar of his talents.

CHAPTER NINE

Marina de La Paz, Baja California Sur

The sky looked as ominous as any red tide Zaragosa had ever seen. It was a sunset of blistering chile peppers that reminded him of the huge schools of pelagic crab that washed ashore near his village every year and turned the beach the color of fresh blood. But unlike the real red tide, *el cielo rojo* was a good omen in the evening sky, and he welcomed it as he maneuvered his newly acquired *panga* through the sailboat moorings and out into the open *Bahía de La Paz*. Manolín sat hunched at the bow wearing the new poncho and Marina de La Paz baseball cap the *mecánico*, Carlos, had given him.

Carlos had been overjoyed at meeting the man who'd saved his life. For two hours the men spoke of their lives, and then Zaragosa told of his experience that day at Isla San Jose, and the perfect storm that nearly killed him. He described the towering waves that tormented him the way a pod of orcas torments a helpless sea lion. The way the island shook. How it angered the sea. He considered sharing the secret of the pearl oysters, but instead he paused and motioned toward Manolín.

"The boy is my only family," he told Carlos, "and without a boat, I cannot provide for him."

Carlos wrapped an arm around the old fisherman's shoulders. "Amigo, my boatyard is crowded with old gringo boats whose engines I fix but whose owners have long since died or given up on the lure of Baja. The storage fees add up and are now worth more than the value of the boat. The owners or their relatives have abandoned many of them. You may have your pick."

"A most unexpected kindness," Zaragosa said, "but I cannot afford to maintain such a large boat."

Carlos nodded. "Then it is fortuitous that you saved the life of a future outboard mechanic."

Zaragosa smiled. "A trusty *panga* is more useful to me than the fanciest yacht. It is all I know." He paused. "And it uses less *gasolina*."

"Take my personal *panga*. With all the supplies you need." He saw the surprise in Zaragosa's face and then the hesitation. "It will be an insult if you do not accept my gift to you and your *nieto*."

"A loan only," Zaragosa answered. "Until I can afford to buy another. A few months if the fishing is good." In his mind's eye he exchanged pearling for fishing.

"Then for once I hope the fishing is bad."

Zaragosa acknowledged the gift with a submissive twist of his bearded lips.

"A *panga* is nothing compared to a life," Carlos added. "It is an honor to my family that you take it."

"Thank you, amigo. Such a kindness is most uncommon among the day-to-day struggles of our life."

"Our bond is uncommon."

Zaragosa gripped the mechanic's shoulder. "You owe me nothing, but I will accept this gift and in return I will bring you something precious one day."

The two men hugged, and with Manolín's help soon had the *panga* loaded and launched.

Now, with the city lights in their wake and the islands bathed in the afterglow of the setting sun, Zaragosa relaxed for the first time since his lapse in judgment. The sea was once again a comfort. His home in San Evaristo was only a few hours away, but more importantly, Isla San Jose and the prized pearl oysters were once again on the horizon.

CHAPTER TEN

Magdalena Bay, Baja California Sur

By the time Skegs returned from following the UFC thugs out of town, Fish was gone, and Roscoe and Tawny were drunk on free booze and threatening to swim out to the seaplane and sing "La Bamba" for the tall man with the long goatee and the enormous red-bellied pearl.

"We could sleep on the pontoons," Roscoe slurred to his wife. "How cool would that be?"

"Bad idea," Skegs interrupted.

"Hey, you're the guy we've been waiting for!" Tawny shrieked happily.

"I am?"

"He said you'd take us fishing tomorrow." She glanced around furtively. "Black snook," she whispered, her hooded eyes glazed with tequila.

Skegs sighed. "Did he?"

"Yep," Roscoe said. "Told us you couldn't fish worth a damn, but said you knew where to find 'em."

"Sounds like something he'd say."

"So you'll do it?" Tawny clapped.

"You promise not to swim to his seaplane; I promise to put you on the snook."

"Pinky promise." Tawny hiccupped and reached out a hand.

Roscoe watched them lock pinkies and asked, "How rich *is* that guy?"

"Owns half the bay and most of the islands around here within boating distance. Spends his money to protect them."

Roscoe whistled and lost his balance.

Skegs caught him by the shoulder and said, "You two want a black snook in the morning, you better get to passing out."

He walked them to the parking lot and pointed up the dirt road. "One block. Take a right. It's the only motel in town. You can't miss it. Walls covered in green clovers. Only clovers in Baja. God love the Irish." He saluted and then turned back to his new clients. "See you after breakfast. Sleep in. Tide doesn't turn until midmorning."

As Skegs reentered the bar, the evening sun plunged into the bay and gilded the bay in bronze light. He settled onto a bar stool and drained his beer. He quickly ordered another. Six beers later, he was joined by a pale-faced man with a Canadian accent and a thick wallet. The beers became shots of Macho Mescal, and by ten o'clock, Skegs was telling Fish stories.

"Come on, eh?" the man said skeptically. "He makes shrimp-skin boots?"

Skegs nodded and reached into his pocket. He removed his iPhone and showed the man the photos. "Buffett would be proud," he boasted.

"Warren?"

Skegs pocketed the phone with a scowl. "What's your name again?"

"Angus." He held out his hand. "Angus Black."

"And where are you from, Angus?"

"Canada."

"Canadians have never heard of Jimmy Buffett?"

"I was pulling your leg. Bet you didn't know they were cousins, eh?" Angus asked, and ordered another round. "Jimmy and Warren. Weird, eh?"

"Eh?" Skegs parroted.

Angus smiled. "You like that, eh? It's a Canada thing." He sipped his mescal. "Does this Mr. Fish live around here? I may want to purchase a pair of those one-of-a-kind boots of his." He offered an oversized wink. "Eh?"

Skegs toasted to the joke. "Just so happens he's staying aboard his trawler right out front." Skegs pointed out at the lights of the *Fish Goddess*.

"Alone?" Angus asked, trying not to telegraph his excitement. Swiping the pearl was going to be easier than he thought.

"Just him and Rosie."

"His wife?"

Skegs laughed again. "That'll be the day."

Angus stared at him blankly.

"Guess you're not a fan of Jackson Browne, either."

Angus shrugged. "What about you?"

"I'm a fan."

"No, do you live aboard a boat also?"

"Naw," Skegs said, and downed his shot of mescal. "Got a little piece of oceanfront in La Paz."

"That's quite a drive, eh?"

"Not in my tricked-out Baja ride."

Angus whistled his appreciation. "The one out front, covered in happy worms?"

"Want to join me for a ride around town?"

"Now?"

"After all the free booze, it's the least I can do." He motioned for another round. "We can take the drinks with us."

"Maybe later," Angus said. "Did you build it yourself?"

"Twenty grand for the kit," Skegs heard himself slur, and he blinked, trying to clear his head. He watched the bartender pour the fresh round of shots. She placed them to the bar.

"*Salud,*" she said, and hurried to fill another order.

Skegs gave a glassy smile, but instead of raising the mescal, he unfurled an arm and snatched an iguana into the air.

"Say *hola* to Pancho."

Angus jerked back. "He's tame?"

"My drinking buddy," Skegs said, handing the lizard to Angus.

The Canadian held it stiffly in outstretched arms.

"Cleans up all the spilled booze. He and Lefty." Skegs glanced around. "Who's probably passed out somewhere around here." Skegs downed his shot.

Angus passed back the lizard, and as Skegs leaned down to set him to the floor, the ex-cat burglar reached out a foot and hooked the leg of the salesman's stool. As Skegs started to slip, Angus caught him by the back of the shirt, hauling him upright while snatching his iPhone from his pocket.

"Salud!" Angus said, and hefted his shot glass without drinking it.

Feeling his face flush at the near fall, Skegs squinted at the nautical clock across the bar. "I think I'll hit the hay."

"I thought you lived in La Paz?"

Skegs stood unsteadily. "Not tonight. Got the cot in the back office. Thanks for the drinks."

Angus reached out and shook Skegs's hand. "Maybe I'll see you in the morning, eh?"

Skegs shook his head. "Going fishing," he said. "Don't forget to tell Mr. Fish I recommended the boots. Maybe he'll give you a discount."

As he weaved a path between the tables and disappeared through the office door, Angus dumped the contents of his own shot glass to the sandy floor and headed outside to fire up his accomplices and put into motion his early retirement.

CHAPTER ELEVEN

Magdalena Bay, Baja California Sur

Fish sat at the head of the king-sized bed, a trifecta of pillows supporting his lower back. The small bedside lamp illuminated the yellow bag in his lap. Balanced on outstretched legs was a portable computer. Months earlier, Fish had arranged for the largest cellular service provider in Baja to install a radio-frequency tower on the highest hill between Puerto San Carlos and Ciudad Constitución. It was paid for by Fish and was fashioned into an enormous fake cardón cactus complete with a half-dozen outstretched arms the size of telephone poles.

A shame the UFC boneheads hadn't broken their knuckles on *it* instead of settling on the real one just outside of town, Fish thought as he finished his email to Toozie McGill. He explained the run-in with the three fighters, the confrontation at the bar, the resulting dunking in the shark cage, and then the strange discovery of three magnificently hued pearls. The large crooked beauty and the strange way it pulsed with light. He briefly mentioned the Legend of Mechudo and then signed off with a *Miss you like a dolphin without its pod, like a sea without its gull,* added a smiley face to temper the bad poetics, and hit *send.*

Next he emailed his attorney in La Paz for any update on the purchase of more islands or the interest of the Nature Conservancy to expand their reach beyond Espíritu Santo north into the Sea of Cortez. Then he stretched his arms above his head and looked up at the ceiling and marveled again at the expert craftsmanship of the local carpenters who inlaid the tongue-and-groove slats of salvaged wood sanded to a fine finish and varnished into a deep honey brown.

He smiled at the thought of Toozie sleeping beside him as they cruised the islands soon to be entrusted to perpetual conservation. Then he returned his attention to the computer and began a Google search of Sea of Cortez pearls. For the next hour he read about the Pericú and Yaqui Indians and their free dives deep into the oyster-rich waters of Bahía de La Paz. He learned about the wealth of the early Spanish and Mexican pearlers, the Jesuits, and then the four-hundred-grain Pearl of La Paz presented to the queen of Spain. These had been heady times for the local pearl industry that ended abruptly by the time Steinbeck and Ricketts sailed by in 1940. Overharvesting and disease had all but wiped them out.

Next he searched for information on purple-hued teardrop pearls the size and shape of a snake's head. Nothing—unless farmed pearls were factored in. He found some mention of differently colored pearls in the halcyon days of Baja pearling, but nothing recent. Nothing at all. He found an article about the young diver Mechudo, and then got distracted reading about seeding oysters and manipulating hues. Aided by the lapping of the bay against the hull, his eyes grew heavy until finally his head lolled back against the headboard and the bag holding the pearl spilled from his lap.

As the long day carried him deep into sleep, not even the sound of Skegs's neon Volkswagen roaring to life a few hundred yards away brought him from his slumber.

CHAPTER TWELVE

Puerto San Carlos, Baja California Sur

Angus Black had waited for last call to exit the bar. Behind him, a few late-night stragglers ordered a final cocktail, not likely to notice the pale-faced Canadian step out into the starlight. He padded quietly across the parking lot to Skegs's neon VW Bug and slipped into the driver's seat. Hot-wiring the silly machine would be a simple business. Or, as it happened, entirely unnecessary: When he groped in the dark for the ignition, he saw the rabbit's-foot key chain. Astounded by the owner's trust in his fellow travelers, Angus glanced once around the mostly empty lot and turned the ignition switch.

He winced as the engine rumbled loudly to life, worried that the sound would catch the attention of his intended victim asleep on the boat. He glanced over his shoulder as he sped away, expecting to see a shadow move from the lighted saloon to the back deck. But no shadow moved, and the boat remained motionless. Angus relaxed and returned his focus to the short drive to the outskirts of town where the three UFC hopefuls awaited his arrival.

He'd found them at sunset, after he'd watched the humiliation of the cast net and the spectacle of the shark cage. After it was over, the Indian deckhand had pointed to the way out of town and then followed the exhaust-spewing Winnebago on foot. But "out of town" wasn't far in this one-stop village, and Angus had no trouble finding them less than a mile away.

The fighters were already fuming about revenge when Angus came upon their makeshift camp. Two of them were still dripping with seawater, chugging tequila, and flinging threats into the desert like circus barkers. The young one stood away from his comrades, nursing a soda, his cheeks visibly scratched by the claw marks from the flying lizard. The big guy's head was pocked with red welts, and the other man had reslung his arm with a torn T-shirt. Both looked angry as hornets.

Angus had chosen his words carefully as he offered them a job. He explained how the bar owner had double-crossed him in a business deal. The lie gave the Canadian instant credibility. That, plus the promise of a hundred bucks for luring the barefoot man to the cantina after hours. The fighters needed something to scare the owner off his boat in enough of a panic to abandon the galley unsecured and leave the pearl unguarded. A few well-aimed bottlerockets might do the trick. Or better yet, pitch some M-80's to the top of the palm-thatched roof. Ignite the kindling and watch it burn to the ground.

The getaway would be easy, he told them. Instead of fleeing for the border, something the expatriate would expect, they should head south for La Paz where hiding out in a beat-up Winnebago would be a breeze. Then, for an extra few hundred bucks, he directed them to ferret out a dive shop owner willing to loan out a portable air compressor and reliable scuba gear. They would avoid any of the annoying paperwork or identifications required stateside. It would be a cash deal with no questions asked.

Now, as the witching hour approached, Angus handed the one named Tank the stolen iPhone and a hundred-dollar bill. "I listed my number under the name Sharkey. Call me when you find the dive shop, eh? I might be out of range, so if I don't hear from you, I'll call when I get to the old marina. Google Maps lists it as a place called Marina de La Paz. Two days max, eh?"

"The rest of the money," Tank demanded. "We talked it over, and none of us is in a trusting mood."

"Suit yourself," Angus said, and snatched back the hundred-dollar bill. "Keep the phone as a memento." He turned to walk away.

"Wait," Tank growled. "You better show up in La Paz."

Angus turned back. "Unless my boat sinks, I'll be there." He handed Tank the C-note. "You'll get the other hundred when the dive gear's loaded aboard."

Mikey stepped from the shadows of the Winnebago. "I don't think we need to light the whole place on fire. How about the small palapa opposite the parking lot, where he keeps his mule? That and the explosions will bring him to shore in a hurry, I'm sure."

"Well, I ain't," Tank hissed. "Son of a bitch's gonna pay for what he done to us. Whole damn place is toast."

Mikey backed into the shadows, and thirty minutes later, waited in the driver's seat with the Winnebago's headlights turned off as Tank and Jimbo aimed fireworks at the roof of Cantina del Cielo.

A few hundred yards offshore, Angus Black crouched in his dinghy, awaiting the conflagration. He'd returned the neon Bug to its parking space and hid in the shadows, watching the boat for signs of life. When he saw no movement, he scurried to the waterline where he'd left his dinghy and rowed silently into the bay. He could just make out his stolen sailboat anchored a quarter of a mile down the shoreline. His was closest to the bay's entrance, its anchor light dark, its crooked mast a mere shadow on the horizon. A ten-minute paddle from the lights of the *Fish Goddess,* it would be an easy escape once he'd commissioned the pearl from inside the refurbished trawler.

Angus knew the fireworks would startle the bar owner and bring the sleepy expatriate hurrying ashore to put out the fire—especially knowing his wingman, Skegs, would be passed out in the back. Leaving the trawler unattended. Its doors unlocked.

The magnificent pearl unguarded.

Suddenly, the sky blossomed with flames and bursts of sound. Angus watched the trawler's saloon door fly open and the tall man bound over the stern and into the dinghy. The bar owner pulled against the oars like a man possessed, and within minutes he was sprinting to the sidewall of the bar where he opened the spigot on a garden hose that spit water uselessly on the flames.

Angus rowed to the abandoned *Fish Goddess* and ducked into the shadowy starboard corner at the stern. In the distance, the palapa roof crackled brightly, the owner futilely arcing water onto the lower fronds.

In the burgeoning firelight, Angus could just make out the Winnebago disappearing into the desert. He gave his new business partners an imaginary thumbs-up, then crept aboard the *Fish Goddess* and ducked inside the open saloon door.

CHAPTER THIRTEEN

Puerto San Carlos, Baja California Sur

Fish dropped the garden hose, smashed through the locked front door, and sprinted across the hard-packed sand. Rounding the schooner-planked bar top, he scooped Pancho and Lefty from their bibulous slumber and raced toward his office with a drunken iguana under each arm. Bits of burning palm fronds rained down around him. A driftwood table burst into flames as he passed. Fish ducked into the back office where Skegs lay snoring on the pullout couch.

"Get up!" Fish yelled, and dropped both iguanas to the mescal-maker's chest. "Now!"

Skegs groaned groggily. "I smell smoke."

"Go out the back way."

"If this is some kind of joke—"

"Now, goddammit!"

His friend's tone immediately sobered Skegs. He sat upright, knocking a lizard to the floor. "What about these two?"

"Take them with you."

Skegs held them to his chest like a couple of scaly babies and stumbled from the office.

Fish glanced around him at the many photographs on the walls. Celebrations of his many philanthropic projects around the bay. The opening of the small school refurbished with the expatriate's generous donations. The local cannery employees surrounding the stainless steel tanks with state-of-the-art filters capable of converting fish oil to petrol. The four-wheel-drive Land

Rover painted *Federales*-style and fitted with infrared technology and the newest-generation GPS systems for his amigo, Xavier, the town's only law enforcement officer. A decade of memories now at the mercy of the approaching flames.

His eyes dropped to a small end table that held a leather-wrapped vase engraved with the gratitude of the local townspeople for the tenth anniversary of the popular cantina. A crackling explosion of fire hurried him to the antique desk atop a wooden foundation hidden by a heavy throw rug. Fish shoved the desk into the corner, kneeled to the floorboards, and peeled back the throw rug to reveal the floor safe. Minutes later, he joined Skegs outside on the dirt road behind the cantina, an army surplus bag slung over his shoulder. Behind him the palapa crashed to the ground and erupted into a bonfire.

Skegs turned away from the flames' brightness. "Dude, you have fire insurance?"

"Nope."

"Damn."

The two friends were quiet for a moment. Then Skegs noticed the army surplus satchel over Fish's shoulder. "What in the bag?"

"A million in cash."

"No, really."

Fish set the satchel to the dirt. "I hope Chuy's all right."

"Flew the coop."

"I'm serious."

Skegs pointed toward a palm tree just up the dirt road. A scarlet macaw was perched on a low frond, its colorful feathers sparkling with the reflection of the burning bar.

Fish heaved a sigh of relief.

Skegs returned his attention to the satchel and saw the small padlock. He rubbed the hangover from his eyes. "For real, man. What's in the bag?"

Fish ignored the question. "It's going to be a total loss," he commented, sadness tugging down the edges of his usual optimism.

"It's a good thing then that you've got an extra million lying around," Skegs joked, trying to lighten the mood. He reached into his pockets. "Shit."

Fish waited.

"My wallet and phone. I left them in the office." He stole a glance once again at the satchel. "You got me covered, right?"

"You want me to replace your wallet and phone?"

"And the cash would be cool, too."

Fish's eyes pinched. "How much?"

"Couple grand," Skegs said offhandedly. He kicked a bare foot at the dirt road. "Three, to be exact."

"You were carrying three grand around in your wallet?"

"I don't own an army surplus bag."

Fish allowed a wry grin and reached into the pocket of his sailcloth pants. "Good thing I grabbed it off the floor on my way out." He handed Skegs the thin fabric wallet. "A bit light for three large."

"Thanks," Skegs said unenthusiastically.

"No phone, though. Sorry."

Skegs stared at the smoking wreckage of Cantina del Cielo. "Are you thinking electrical?"

"I heard explosions. Fireworks."

Skegs jerked his head around with a start and regretted it, a sneak preview of the morning's hangover rocking him. He rubbed at his temples and asked, "Shit, man, you think it was those UFC cats who torched the joint?"

Fish nodded.

"Motherfuckers."

Fish tugged at his braided goatee, his eyes closed, his breath short and sharp. Skegs could see the tall man's jaw set tightly, the muscles of his neck twitchy with anger.

"I know what you're thinking, hoss. But for once let the cops handle it."

Fish was silent. He slowly opened his eyes, his fingers remaining on the metal crimp holding the tail of his goatee, his face flat.

Skegs stepped back. "Not liking the look in your eyes, partner."

"People depend on this place for their livelihood. Isabela, Mamacita, the local community—they all get a boost from the visitors."

"So use some of that cash to set a world-record rebuild."

"Already planning it."

"It's the other plan I'm worried about."

"Don't."

"Listen, man, the last time you tried to play hero, you took two bullets. The time before that, I almost got popped by that Chula Vista Chicano freak. Our close-call quotient be running low."

"Third time's the charm."

"I'm serious, man."

"These fools aren't armed. They're thickheaded bullies. I've never cared much for bullies. Not in the courtroom and not on the beach."

"So we call Xavier. He'll track down that crappy Winnebago in no time with the new wheels you bought him."

"Xavier's in Cabo guarding the governors at their annual convention. By the time he gets free, those guys will be across the border."

"They're not worth it, man."

"We can't just let them walk."

"What do you mean, *we*?"

"Are you or are you not my wingman?"

Skegs kicked the satchel and felt the heaviness of the bundled money. "You weren't kidding about the million bucks, were you?"

Fish bent low and hefted the satchel without answering. "Seaplane flies on fish oil."

Skegs shrugged. "I know that. So what?"

"Two tanks filled with the stuff."

Skegs gave him a puzzled look.

"Pilots can dump fuel in midflight." He winked at his friend. "For safety reasons, of course."

Skegs started to smile. "No hand-to-hand combat bullshit. Just a little flyover to add a little stinky sheen to a trio of fleeing dirtbags. I like it."

"Nothing reckless about it."

"They'll be racing for the border."

"Most likely."

"Easy to spot from the air."

"Yep."

"Only one road to the border."

Fish gave a thumbs-up.

Again Skegs massaged his temples. "No crazy white man shit like bouncing a pontoon off their windshield, right?"

"Right."

"Swear on it."

"What, are we Boy Scouts now?"

Skegs raised his brow and waited.

"I swear on it."

"If my head didn't hurt, I'd hug you."

Fish started toward the parking lot. "Plane's low on fuel. Cannery's got a fresh batch cooked up and ready to go in fifty-five-gallon drums." He stole a glance at the neon-green Volkswagen Bug. "I hate to ask, but—"

"You need a race-car driver to get you there fast," Skegs finished the sentence. He started jogging toward the car, and then slowed to a stop.

"Don't tell me," Fish said, catching up. "You left the keys in the office."

Skegs held up a palm, turned, and emptied his stomach onto the dirt. He straightened and wiped the back of his hand across his mouth. "You should have a talk with whoever makes that mescal you've been selling. Strong shit."

"Preaching to the choir, amigo." He held out his hand for the keys. "I'll drive."

"Good idea."

Fish waited.

"What?"

"Keys."

"Come on, man. This is Baja. Keys are in the ignition."

CHAPTER FOURTEEN

Magdalena Bay, Baja California Sur

Angus Black worked quickly. A cat burglar by trade, he'd fled his home country of Canada after a grainy video was broadcast on *Canada's Most Wanted*. Angus had pinched the jewels from a posh condo in Vancouver's art district on what was forecast to be a cloudy evening. Unfortunately, as he descended the thick blanket of ivy at the back of the building, the clouds parted to reveal a spectacular full moon—more than enough light for the security cameras. Angus immediately pawned the gems and fled across the U.S. border into Washington.

Unfamiliar with the territory, he branched out into nab and grabs. Purses, high-end shopping bags, briefcases, and computer bags. But after a failed strong-arm robbery left him with a dislocated shoulder, he hitchhiked to Berkeley. His arm too sore to work the crowds, he waited until after midnight and then pulled a switchblade on a five-foot Asian man in jeans and a sport coat.

"Your wallet or your life," he growled in his best Clint Eastwood.

The skinny man bowed kindly and kept walking. Angus reached out with his good arm and grabbed a bony shoulder. It was the last thing he remembered. That and the searing pain from a badly broken thumb.

Another week of hitchhiking found him just short of Mexico, in the liberal enclave of Ocean Beach, California, where a group of well-tanned homeless men welcomed him into their panhandling circuit. Days of blissful begging ended when the group suspected

Angus of keeping more than his share of the daily bounty. They were right to. Instead of pooling his donations to the community booze fund, Angus was skimming for his own needs. Food and sunscreen. Mostly sunscreen. The confrontation ended with Angus leaping into the moonlit water at Dog Beach and swimming to the jetty, where he disappeared, ghostlike, into the night.

He took refuge near the Mission Bay Marina and awoke staring at a forest of boat masts. For the first time in his life he felt a desire to do more than steal. Maybe it was the balmy nights and the pleasant water temperature of his starlit swim the night before, but Angus was suddenly, and powerfully, drawn to this briny southern sea—a far cry from the icy northern shores of his past.

And so, that night during the witching hours just before dawn, he broke into a dusty, guano-covered twenty-two-foot sailboat with a crooked mast. Its cranky outboard motor started after some well-aimed strikes to the cowling and a few-dozen lumberjack-like pulls on the starter cord. As a gray light began to distinguish the jetty of two nights earlier, Angus motored out to sea in the stolen sailboat. The outside of the craft may have been neglected, but inside it held a treasure trove of sailing books and charts and enough canned food to last a month. Canned food and a drawer filled with an assortment of sunscreen. Tubes of the white stuff in copious amounts. So much sunscreen that Angus considered it a godsend for a man of his complexion. As a Canadian, he feared sunburn so intensely that the theft of the sailboat suddenly seemed more an entitlement than a crime. A kind of karmic reboot of his life as he headed south of the border.

For three months, Angus traveled south along Baja's western shoreline, slathering himself with the sunblock and learning the feel of the waves and the wind. He read every seafaring book from cover to cover, and remained close to shore as he learned to sail. He pulled into each successive marina, but only at night, and only long enough to canvas the docks and appropriate any unsecured bounty from the decks of the American yachts. Though they gated marinas to keep landlubbers and thieves on shore, boaters seemed to have an unreasonable trust in other boaters. Decks brimmed with all sorts of expensive contraband, and by the time Angus pulled into Magdalena Bay's Puerto San Carlos, he'd accumulated a boatload of handheld radios, small outboard engines, fishing reels, cases of motor oil, and an assortment of wallets and purses filled with almost five thousand dollars in American cash.

But nothing matched the enormous teardrop pearl he'd seen earlier that evening. Even the clearly well-seasoned bar owner had been captivated by its beauty. Now, as Angus searched the master stateroom, he felt his pulse race. He had intimate knowledge of all the common hiding places, all the futile attempts at amateur camouflage. He also knew that the bar owner had not expected to race off in the middle of the night. He knew that the shock of hearing the explosions and then seeing his bar on fire would trump all thoughts of hiding the yellow bag with the pearl. Angus was certain the prize would be left in the open, or at worst in a bureau drawer or a jewelry case.

The one-time cat burglar risked turning off the bedside lamp to hide his shadow. All eyes would be on the inferno. Then he freed a penlight from his trousers, cupped his palm over it, and swept the thin beam across the room. He scanned the bedside table, freed the top drawer, the unmade bed. Nothing. As he made his way toward the master head, the penlight flashed over a corner of yellow plastic. It was on the floor, of all places, beside a fallen pillow. He lifted the pillow and saw the yellow bag. He snatched it and felt the weight of the pearl inside, took a deep, satisfied breath, and flicked off the penlight.

"First rule of wealth management," he whispered with a gleeful grin. "Never sleep with the finery."

He hurried back outside to the deck and slipped into the dinghy, and twenty minutes later hopped to the stern of his pirated sailboat. He pulled anchor and started the small outboard engine with a single well-practiced pull for the short ride to open water, then hoisted the sail up the crooked mast and caught the starlit breeze.

Patience and timing, he reminded himself. That was when great things happened to the chosen ones. He'd avoided the Canadian Mounties, the San Diego gang of hobos, found a boat seemingly made for him, and then sailed into a dream state of easy pickings, only to come across a curiously popular bar in the middle of nowhere with a bag of treasure. It was a series of events unthinkable just a few months earlier. And there he'd been, sitting within earshot of the pearl conversation. It was more than just dumb luck. It was destiny, pure and simple.

A cocksure smile pulled at his lips as he thought back to the fortuitous conversation.

The couple had told the bar owner that they'd found the bag of pearls on a rocky outcropping at Isla San Jose. A yellow plastic grocery bag clinging to the barnacles. Angus saw it as proof that the once-famed oyster beds were flourishing, and that a local fisherman had probably made the discovery. If the expatriate was correct, Angus knew that the fisherman would return to the proving grounds for more pearls. Unshelling a pearl was no different than unearthing a diamond or a vein of gold. The fever would spread, and the mass harvesting would begin in earnest. When it did, Angus planned to be there with his thousands in purloined cash.

Angus lathered his skin with sunscreen in anticipation of sunrise. Then he opened one of the well-worn Baja books and found San Evaristo, the nearest village to the island. But Angus didn't need a village. He needed a city.

A city with dive shops and an owner with suspect ethics.

A city like La Paz.

CHAPTER FIFTEEN

La Paz, Baja California Sur

Bartholomew Kraken stood just over five feet tall with cinderblock shoulders and a face marred by a bad temper and a penchant for knife fights. He leaned against the cracked glass counter of his La Paz dive shop and watched the young couple arguing on the sidewalk outside the shop door. His stringy black hair was so thin it hung like threads over his forehead. He puffed air upward and cleared it from his brow, his mismatched eyes narrowing as he willed the couple to enter his shop.

Kraken hadn't had a customer all morning, and by lunchtime he had all but given up—until the young American couple stopped outside the grimy glass doors of Diving Dudes. Kraken had come up with the name in anticipation of finding a partner.

The truth was he'd never scuba dived in his life. Not officially. A couple of YouTube videos, some stolen equipment, and a solo dive from the beach were enough to make him an expert in his own mind. Not that the licensing bureaucrats in La Paz gave a damn. They were desperate for any kind of revenue, now that the tourism industry had been guillotined by the perceived nationwide drug-cartel violence—perceived because Baja so far seemed impervious to the bloody tide of beheadings. So Kraken bought a secondhand business license, hung a sign, and tried to make his stolen money last.

Stolen in the ethical sense, not the legal one—a technicality Kraken felt proud to revisit in his mind often. Kraken was pretty sure stealing ten thousand dollars of counterfeit money was not a crime. Since the money wasn't legal to begin with, how could it be illegal to steal? Freshly printed by old man Denis, a banknote artist of acclaim in certain San Diego circles and Kraken's boss for most of the past ten years. A decade of stamping out counterfeit paper, until one day the old man got careless. Maybe it was a stroke. Or maybe it was the daily morning routine of vodka added a bit too liberally to the coffee cup. Not that it mattered. He'd seriously mangled both his hands, and mangled hands required explanation—an explanation that, if truthful, would surely lead to prison.

So as Kraken rushed the old man to the emergency room, he agreed to hide the heavy printer out back under a tarp and quickly replace it with a store-bought lathe—some kind of Home Depot special. Kraken would transfer the old man's blood and bone fragments to the lathe and hope the health and safety inspector bought it during his inevitable visit. Hope he didn't notice the decade of ink indelibly staining the garage cement floor, or the unmistakable smell of freshly inked linen, and feel compelled to direct the cops' interest to the business's *real* business.

But halfway back to the El Cajon garage, Kraken had an epiphany. He also had an aversion to interrogations, especially when his partner in crime was an addled old man on pain medication. Their two stories would never hold up, and Kraken would take the fall. Prison was hard enough for average-height criminals. For a man as short and wide as Kraken, it would be unbearable. The endless fireplug ridicule. The constant fighting to defend his honor and prove his courage. And then there were the eyes. One was almost black; the other a stark white. A birthmark of sorts. Distracting at best.

A fist-magnet most likely.

So instead of switching out machines after dropping the old man off, Kraken parked out front of his nondescript suburban house, left the truck running, hurried into the garage, loaded paper grocery bags with bundles of counterfeit bills, packed his few belongings, and headed south. Away from curious investigators and prying neighbors. Someplace where his hundreds would be easily laundered.

A place like Baja California.

He crossed into Tijuana that night and drove straight through to Baja's largest city, La Paz, a place where he could relax and plan for the future. For six months he lived out of his truck and wandered the dusty streets, drinking bottled *ballenas* of beer wrapped in newspaper and hanging out with the local expatriates. Most were drunks living off social security or pension plans, but one semi-sober retiree ran a charter fishing business from an old catamaran docked at one of the favorite expat hangouts, Marina de La Paz. It was a thirty-two-footer named *Reel Cool,* a fishing boat with fewer and fewer customers, what with tourists avoiding Mexico like schools of squid avoiding the sunlight. Which was the topic of conversation one night over Tecates and tacos.

"The fishing business is drying up," he told Kraken after replacing their beers with heavy slugs of rum in plastic Dixie cups. "Between the goddamn commercial guys taking all the game fish, and the drug cartels cutting off everyone's head, I'm lucky to get one charter a week. And that's *with* the cheapest rates in town."

"Branch out," Kraken said between sips of rum.

"Ain't a thing to branch out into."

"There's a crapload of little colorful fish swimming around the islands out there. How about scuba-diving charters?"

"Never done it."

"You know how to breathe, don't you?"

Two hours later they struck a deal. Kraken would set up shop in town, and the old man would add a banner to his dock. *Reel Cool Diving Dudes.* A fifty-fifty split after fuel and food was deducted. That was two months ago, and since then they'd had only two diving charters. Desperation was setting in as fast as Kraken's phony money was running out.

Kraken needed a hell of a lot more than just this young couple's business, but it would be better than nothing. If they'd only come inside. The young woman outside the shop was shaking her head angrily, and the man was talking and gesturing with his hands. But then all at once the argument seemed to stop. She finally shrugged and he yanked open the door for her, jangling the little bell.

Still the young woman paused, and Kraken had to admire her ability to read the subtle signs of his despair. She was smart to be hesitant, but the man, dulled by an adventurer's pride or a youthful stubbornness, charged ahead, knocking the bell from its flimsy wire, and the woman reluctantly followed him inside.

Dust covered the smattering of equipment strewn around the cramped room, kept cool by the constant whir of an overhead fan. Kraken stepped away from the counter and into the single dim overhead light.

"Looking for a dive?"

The couple stiffened at the sound of his voice, then unconsciously clung to each other at the unsettling sight of him.

"We didn't see you back there," the young man said, watching warily as the Napoleonic man with the albino eye moved closer.

"I keep the lights low to help cool the place."

The woman wiped sweat from beneath her salon-bleached bangs. "Do you give scuba lessons? My boyfriend wants to learn how to dive."

"Hundred bucks apiece to dive the sea mount. Famous place where Jacques Cousteau used to film movies."

They stared blankly.

"Famous French guy. Invented the word scuba."

"Oh," they said in an unimpressed chorus.

"I'll throw in ham sandwiches and free beer."

"Righteous!" The man pumped his fist in the air and turned to the woman. "See, honey? I told you it would be worth it."

"Don't we have to start in a pool first?" the woman asked. He could see her trying to focus on his more normal eye, but her gaze kept drifting toward the white eye. Everybody's did.

"Pools are for pussies," Kraken informed them.

"You mean we can go straight to the ocean?" The man's tone quickened with excitement. "Without a license or nothing?"

Kraken nodded. He combed a dirty hand across his threadbare head and showed a set of neglected teeth. "Nobody gives a damn about a license down here. Too hot. Just remember to breathe. You hold your breath and we got a problem."

"What kind of problem?" the woman asked with alarm.

"Breathe and you won't have to worry about it."

"Sounds easy enough," the man agreed, and yanked a rusty speargun from a nearby rack. "Who'd forget to breathe?"

"Careful," Kraken warned. "That thing's loaded."

The man carefully set it point-first to the floor.

"Two hundred cash." Kraken glanced at his counterfeit dive watch. "*Vámanos*. Before the tide changes and the sharks get too aggressive."

"Sharks?" the woman asked.

"Cool," the man chimed in.

"Hammerheads. That's why we bring along the persuader." When the woman just blinked at him, he pointed at the loaded speargun in the man's hands. "Shot a big one last week. Wanted to bring it back for the taco-stand guys, but the blood kicked off a fucking feeding frenzy. Nothing left but a skeleton by the time we had to surface."

"Nothing left but cartilage, I think you mean," the woman said. She turned to her boyfriend. "Honey, maybe we should talk about this."

Kraken began to speak, but the man dug ten twenties out of his wallet and slapped them on the dusty counter. "Let's go swim with the sharks."

CHAPTER SIXTEEN

Magdalena Bay, Baja California Sur

After flying north in their unsuccessful search for the shoddy
Winnebago, Fish and Skegs returned to Cantina del Cielo to pick
up Mephistopheles and by midday were back at the sand-dune
island and the towering octagon house overlooking both watery
shorelines. Fish landed the seaplane on the calm surface of the
back bay and secured it to its permanent mooring. Then the two
friends transferred to the waiting dinghy and drove fifty yards
to the marled beach of shells and sand. Two Labrador retrievers,
accustomed to the sound of the plane's twin propellers, bounded
down the clamshell path to greet them.

As Fish hauled the dinghy above the tide line, Skegs scratched
the dogs' heads in tandem, and then flung a bat-sized piece of
driftwood into the bay. Both dogs crashed into the clear water and
raced after the floating prize.

"Let's eat," Skegs said, turning from the water. "All this failed
revenge makes me hungry."

Fish wiped his hands on his sailcloth pants and said, "I've got
fresh corvina marinating up top."

They followed the path through the dunes to a sandy yard
planted with succulents and cacti and a forest of baby mesquite
and ironwood trees. The sun was high overhead, reflecting off the
three-story home's ranks of porthole windows. Solar grids lined
the eaves of the palapa roof, and a series of small windmills whirled
soundlessly atop the thatched roof. As the two men approached
the accordion door of the antique-red phone booth that had

washed ashore at Malarrimo Beach and now served as the main entranceway to the great room, a black-and-white-spotted mule appeared from a gap in the sand dunes.

"That ugly old thing ever going to die?" Skegs sneered.

"I hope not," Fish answered, and freed the lid of a tin letter box nailed to the reinforced frame of the telephone booth. The box was filled with brown sugar cubes. He fed Mephistopheles a handful of the sweet treats while Skegs tossed one to each dog before it could stop and shake the bay water from its coat.

Both men entered and crossed the driftwood floor set into a tight herringbone pattern, and then climbed the circular three-story iron staircase that coiled around the redwood center beam like an enormous spring. The redwood, sunk twenty feet deep and buttressed with over a thousand pounds of concrete, served as the unmovable anchor to the oddly shaped house. Fish had designed the eight walls to repel the ever-moving tons of sand that inched across the island like dune-backed centaurs.

They passed the rope-bridge catwalks leading into eight separate rooms and emerged onto the top floor overlooking the expanse of shimmering blue Pacific. The breeze cooled the midday air and ruffled the tips of the dried fronds held tight to the roof with a retired nylon drift net roped into place around hand-hewn beams of mesquite.

"Man, I don't get it," Skegs said, helping himself to a cold beer from the old-fashioned coffin cooler with a Coca-Cola insignia. "How does a crappy old Winnebago disappear like that?"

"It didn't disappear. It went south. That's the only explanation that makes any sense."

"Cabo?"

"That's my guess." Fish hung the seaplane keys from a peg and rooted in the cooler for a cold Fresca. Then he went to the picnic table centered with a view of the water and took a long drink.

Skegs wandered across the veranda, opened the cacti-ribbed pantry, and searched for Mamacita's twice-baked tortillas. "You planning to fuel up and go back after them?"

"Too crowded down south for a fuel dump."

"Good, 'cause I know all the cops in Cabo." He found the tortillas, rolled one into a cigar shape, and ate it dry like a carrot. "I'll make a call."

"I was thinking we could drive," Fish said.

"Ah, man. You already kicked their asses twice. I know you're mad. They burned down your bar. But my buddies in Cabo'll find them and toss their arsonist asses in jail." He washed down the tortilla with the end of the beer. "And that's way more scary than a barefoot dude with a weird goatee and a machete."

"I need something appraised."

"In Cabo?"

"La Paz."

Skegs's eyes widened as he liberated a fresh beer from the cooler. "What kind of something we talking about?"

"A pearl."

Skegs spit up a mouthful of beer.

Fish gave him a weary look. "Round thing. The size of a marble usually."

"I know what pearls are, but nobody gets them *appraised*."

"This one's different. Purplish. Huge and oddly shaped. I think it's from the ancient strain near La Paz."

Skegs's face drained of its color. "The Mechudo pearls?"

"You know about the Legend of Mechudo?"

"Know about it? Jesus, man, it's hammered into every local kid's head. Don't fuck with the church or the bad mojo gonna take you down."

"It's a very old legend."

"Old and deadly." He cleansed his palate with a gulp of beer. "Forget the appraisal, we're heading straight for Our Lady of La

Paz Cathedral. Gonna save somebody's life and turn the bad mojo into something good."

"It's not mine to give away."

Skegs leaned forward, staring hard at Fish. "Since when did you give a damn about pearls?"

Fish cut slices from a fresh mango and offered a piece to Skegs. "The couple from yesterday said they found them in a plastic bag washed up on the rocks at Isla San Jose."

"Them?"

"Three. Two small ones, one big one."

"And they were in a plastic bag?" he asked skeptically.

Fish nodded.

"And they just gave the biggest pearl to you?"

"I offered to pay for the appraisal. In case they're from the Mechudo strain."

"Let's have a look," Skegs said excitedly.

"It's back on the *Fish Goddess*."

Skegs's face dropped.

"What?" Fish asked.

"Last night," Skegs began slowly, thinking as he spoke. "A pale-faced dude with a funny accent." He paused. "Canadian accent. He was hanging around the bar. He chatted me up and then started asking questions about you. Personal stuff that didn't seem like a big deal at the time. He's the one who bought me all those drinks."

"So?"

"As I remember it, he seemed overly interested in our living arrangements."

"*Our* living arrangements?"

Skegs set his beer to the picnic table and sighed heavily. "He wanted to know if you were alone out on the trawler, and he asked me if I was staying aboard with you or if I was on another boat."

Fish absently twirled the tip of his braided goatee as he considered the information. "This guy just picked you randomly out of the crowd last night?"

"Yep. The minute I got back from following the fighters out of town."

Fish tossed the paring knife to the table and started for the door.

"Son of a bitch was in on the fire!" Skegs yelled, and hurried after him.

"I think he set the whole thing up."

"A hell of a lot of work for a pearl," Skegs offered meekly.

"It's a hell of a pearl," Fish said, then grabbed the keys to the seaplane and headed for the back bay.

CHAPTER SEVENTEEN

Puerto San Carlos, Magdalena Bay

Roscoe and Tawny awoke late with deadly hangovers. After a hasty continental breakfast of dry toast and coffee, they stumbled from Hotel Brennan into the harsh morning sunlight.

"Let's go back to bed," Roscoe grumbled.

Tawny slipped on a pair of sunglasses. "No chance, cowboy. I see black snook on the horizon."

Roscoe hastily shoved sunglasses over his eyes and looked out at the corner of the bay. "At least it's calm." He unzipped his fanny pack to check on the two pearls, then found a sandy stick of lip balm and applied it liberally to his lips.

They began a slow stroll down the dirt street to the corner of the block, turned toward the shoreline, and stopped.

"Oh my God," Tawny said.

"No way," Roscoe added.

"The bar's gone."

"I never heard a fire engine."

"Town this size, I doubt they have one."

"Damn."

They hurried to the charred remains of Cantina del Cielo and watched the old cook rummaging through the ashes. Mamacita found an iron skillet and grinned.

"I love those things," Tawny commented.

Roscoe didn't respond. He recognized the younger woman standing off to the side, her eyes puffy with emotion. He walked up to her.

"You're the coolest bartender in Baja," Roscoe said in broken Spanish. "I'm sure he'll rebuild."

She wiped her eyes. "Yes, but it was so perfect."

"I'm sorry."

"*Gracias.*"

"Is everyone okay?"

Isabela nodded. In broken English she said, "It happened after we closed. Mr. Fish saved the iguanas. And Skegs."

Roscoe sighed with relief. "Are they around?"

She pointed to the mesquite trees and the makeshift stable with its mini-palapa. Two full-sized iguanas lounged in the sun at the top of the palm-frond roof.

"I mean Skegs and Fish," Roscoe explained.

Isabela shook her head. "They left early this morning."

Roscoe's face dropped.

"It's okay. They'll be back next week or so. You and *su esposa* stay and help us rebuild, no?"

"Where did they go?"

She looked at him quizzically.

"Fish and Skegs."

"San Evaristo."

"His bar burns down and he drives to San Evaristo? It's nothing but a fishing village."

She directed his eyes out at the bay. "No driving, señor. Mr. Fish took the big boat."

Roscoe scowled, a sudden knot forming in his stomach. "That doesn't make any sense. Why wouldn't he take his seaplane?"

"Mr. Fish is a friend of yours?"

"What?"

"You and Atticus are amigos?"

"No, um, yes." He thanked her with an awkward hug and hurried back to Tawny, who was talking with Mamacita. "We gotta go."

"I want to stay and help them. Mamacita says we can stay with her. Free room and board." She flashed a grin. "You know how good she can cook."

"We can't."

"What? Why?"

"They're headed back to San Evaristo. With our most valuable pearl, dammit!"

Tawny pulled him to the side. "Slow down. Who's headed to San Evaristo?"

"Fish and his accomplice. They took his trawler."

"But the bar," Tawny protested. "And the snook."

"We'll help later." Roscoe had a wild look in his eyes. "The snook aren't going anywhere. Fish and his buddy are headed for the island! I'll just bet you they tracked down the fisherman who found the pearls. Damn double-crossers!"

"I don't care about the pearls," Tawny said flatly. "I like it here. The people are nice and the bay is gorgeous. Let's explore."

"Please," Roscoe begged. "That pearl belongs to us. I want it back. Then we'll fish for snook. Until you catch one. I promise."

She took a long, disapproving look at the expression that had taken over his face. "Roscoe," she said, "you know they don't really belong to us."

"What do you mean? We found the yellow bag!"

"They belong to whoever put them in that yellow bag."

"But they *lost* them. That's what *losing* something means! And we *found* it, which makes us . . ." Finally absorbing the look she was giving him, he sighed and shut down.

"Which makes us the people who should give them back," she said. "And we don't even know these guys, this Fish and Skegs, but people here sure seem to like them."

"*Like* them," Roscoe said. "They could be lovable as all hell, but once you put a big-ass pearl in someone's pocket and give them a head start toward a bed full of *more* pearls where those came from . . ."

She was giving him the look again. He sighed and again tapped the brakes in his head. "Hell, honey," he went on, trying to sound reasonable, "they could be heading for La Paz to sell it, for all we know. None of this makes sense. His bartender said they were going to San Evaristo. I don't buy it. Why head to a little bitty village within hours of his bar burning down?"

"I'll admit it sounds a little suspect."

He brightened. "There you go. I love you, baby."

"Unless the best palapa builders live in San Evaristo."

Roscoe considered this, then shook his head. "The guy owns a seaplane. Why waste time and take the boat?"

Tawny shrugged.

Roscoe gripped her arm. "Doesn't matter why. What matters is that they *did* take the boat, and it'll take them two days to get there. If we leave now, we can pull in by midafternoon."

Tawny narrowed her eyes, then sighed. "You owe me."

"Do I ever," Roscoe agreed, and raced toward the Land Cruiser they left parked in the lot overnight.

CHAPTER EIGHTEEN

Pacific Ocean, Baja California Sur

The *Fish Goddess* chugged through the rolling swells at eight knots, a comfortable cruising speed for the fifty-two-foot trawler with a shark cage and a mini-submarine lashed to the back deck. Fish had wanted to break down the shark cage for easier transport, but Skegs needed the extra storage. Remorseful that his tequila-loosened tongue had led to the loss of the big pearl and his best friend's cantina, Skegs besieged Fish with demands to pay for the palapa rebuild. Fish refused. Skegs persisted.

So they compromised. Without the pearl, Fish no longer needed the appraisal. Instead, he planned to head straight for Isla San Jose to search for the pearl bed—from the seat of his personal sub. Skegs, however, wanted to stop in Cabo San Lucas to sell his newest batch of Macho Mescal and donate the five thousand dollars to the burned-out-palapa cause. Fish didn't need the money, but Skegs needed the boost to his dignity.

"Only a pit stop," Fish warned. "That's all the time I'm spending in that bacchanal."

"Bacca-huh?" Skegs said.

"Lascivious carnival."

"Hey, you're talking about my job security."

And with that they'd loaded the shark cage with booze—fifty cases of bootleg mescal. Then they made arrangements with the bartender, Isabela, to care for Mephistopheles and the two Labradors. Fish gave her a key to the house and an envelope filled with enough hundreds to pay for the start of the cantina cleanup. An extra few hundred for her and Mamacita's loss of work.

Then they retrieved the submarine from its camouflaged hiding place at the end of a thick mangrove channel, and motored out of Magdalena Bay in the late afternoon, their mood dampened by the events of the last twelve hours. Revenge against the UFC wannabes was no longer a priority. Nor was the pale-faced thief who most likely staged the fire and boarded the *Fish Goddess* to steal the pearl. Skegs would report the Winnebago to his cop friends, who would sooner or later arrest the fighters. As for the Canadian, Fish decided to leave vengeance to karma. In the meantime, he planned to find the oyster bed and save it from extinction. And along the way, find the true owner of the pearls and pay him to donate the first one to the church, thereby extinguishing the malediction of Mechudo.

Fish knew that finding the pearl-producing oyster bed would be almost impossible. But the magnetic energy pulsating inside the large crooked pearl had made his heart pound. He'd long ago given up on poltergeists and phantoms. Drunken fantasies about Shangri-La were things of the past. Yet something about that pearl had touched him in a way never imagined. He couldn't explain it. It felt both visceral and otherworldly, which should have been a warning sign. Rather, it drew him forward on an irresistible quest, as if the fiery core of the margarite had changed him somehow.

He pushed away these troubling thoughts to focus instead on the need to save the fragile oyster bed. Pearling was like strip-mining—the more raw materials harvested, the better the chance of the miners hitting the jackpot. But strip-mining an oyster bed ended all prospects of future oysters—and future pearls. It was the paradox that confronted all harvesters of the ocean's species. Take too much and the species weakens or worse. It was happening to the world's tuna, shark, cod, and the endless list of other targeted table fare. It happened to Chile's sardine population, which in turn ended their offshore swordfish population. And in the Sea of

Cortez, it happened to the pearl oysters. Centuries of clear-cutting miles of oyster beds from Mulegé to La Paz left the beds weakened and vulnerable, allowing the blight to set in, and the great harvest to collapse.

But Fish knew he had an advantage over anyone else searching for the oysters. And it wasn't just time and money. Skegs called it the *Batfish Boogie*. Fish's one-man personal submarine.

"Dude, that's the ugliest sailboat I've ever seen," Skegs said, bringing Fish out of his reverie. He pointed from the helm where the two men stood and directed Fish's attention toward shore. "Its mast is all fucked up."

Fish followed his friend's gaze to where a ragged sailboat paralleled the beach. "Probably some old-timer."

"Crazy coot's more like it. A norther blows through and that guy's toast."

"Takes all kinds down here," Fish said. "Todos Santos is on the horizon."

"Eight hours to Cabo," Skegs said excitedly. "Want to slow down and troll for a bit?"

"And roll in to Cabo at midnight? That's crazy."

Skegs gave him an impatient look. "Better than rolling in at happy hour. We might even have time to chill for a bit at a favorite hangout."

"I'm in a hurry."

"Shit, man, this is Baja. Ain't no hurry in the vocab."

"You know what I mean."

"What I know is you can buy all the pearls you want with what's in that army surplus bag of yours." He watched his friend look away. "Come on, man. I get the island thing. Stopping the developers and shit. But pearls. What the hell? They farm pearls like shrimp these days."

"They were extraordinary."

"You need a shot of reality, brother. At the end of the day, pearls are nothing more than hardened oyster snot."

Fish didn't say anything.

"This isn't about the pearls, is it?"

"It's about saving something meaningful. Greedy colonists wiped out one of the world's great pearl beds. We can do something about it. Not many people have a chance to preserve something so rare that was harvested to extinction."

"Harvesting a wild fish for dinner sounds meaningful to me."

"We've got filets in the freezer."

"And babes galore in Cabo. Might take your mind off the pearls for a while."

"One hour is what you get. If you're not back, I'm not waiting."

Skegs dropped his head. "I said I was sorry." He brushed back a kelplike strand of hair. "I know I screwed everything up, but I'm on your side. You're like a brother. I just want to make things right."

Fish sighed. "Slow her down."

"Really?"

"Really."

"I love you, man!" Skegs hollered happily, and raced belowdecks for his fishing gear.

CHAPTER NINETEEN

San Evaristo, Baja California Sur

It was late when Zaragosa ran the *panga* up the beach near his one-room shack. The village was quiet and the dirt street empty of life. The sky hung heavy with stars. Manolín shuffled beside his grandfather and within minutes was asleep in his small bed, the Mexican blanket tucked around him.

Zaragosa lit the small gas stove and placed a pan with water over the burner. He waited for the water to boil, and then removed the pan and added a heavy spoonful of coffee grounds. A phantom sugar bowl sat on the plywood table next to the stove, and he pretended to scoop the sweetener into his ceramic cup, its cracked handle glued where it periodically snapped free after its collision with the floorboard of his *panga*.

Zaragosa took the steaming cup out to the sandy yard and thought about his old *panga* lying somewhere on the bottom of the ocean. He wondered if the animals had taken shelter under its fiberglass hull, or whether the outboard engine he'd fixed so many times had broken free of the transom and lay sideways in the rocks, collecting barnacles. It saddened his heart when he thought of the boat all alone in the cold blackness. And then he remembered the young skin diver, Mechudo, and the greed that led to his death. Maybe Mechudo stood at the underwater stern like so many drowned pirates, his long black hair flowing with excitement as he circled the oyster bed.

Zaragosa knew how close he had come to drowning—how close Manolín had come to losing his only family. Never again, the old man vowed. He would harvest only enough pearls to better their lives. The first would go to the local church in a public display of faith and deference. In the name of Mechudo, so his ghost could rest in peace. So his family could finally have comfort.

And it was this public knowledge that would threaten the oyster bed and Zaragosa's claim to it. No secrets could be held forever. And even if he tried, he would eventually be discovered when selling his pearls in La Paz. Even if he sold them elsewhere, he'd draw attention for not fishing yet drawing a steady income.

He drank the strong coffee and knew he'd have to tell someone soon. Before the rumors spread. Before he was followed.

Before anyone got hurt.

CHAPTER TWENTY

Desierto, Baja California Sur

As dawn brightened into day, Roscoe sped down the dirt road like a driver fleeing arrest. The skiff tied to the Land Rover's roof rack rattled loudly, and the supplies stacked in the backseat had toppled across the seats and the floorboards.

"Halt!" Tawny yelled.

Roscoe reluctantly slowed. "Halt?"

"Yeah, like stop the car! You're going to wreck us if you don't slow down." She pointed out the window. "And I'm pretty sure I just saw a cow out there with a car door around its neck."

Roscoe stopped the car and blinked through the dusty windshield, seeing nothing. "Maybe you're still drunk from last night."

"Speak for yourself, kettle."

"A cow with a car-door necklace? That's drunk talk."

Tawny glared at him. "It was back there, speed demon."

"Okay, I'll slow down."

"What about the cow?"

"Must have been a mirage," he offered, and started to accelerate.

"It wasn't a mirage."

"We're not wrangling some cow out in the middle of the desert to save it from a collar some rancher put around its neck for some reason we know nothing about. That's the rancher's business." He inched up the speedometer, hoping she wouldn't notice.

"I want a photo."

Roscoe reluctantly stopped. "Have at it, cowgirl," he said.

Tawny grabbed her camera and exited the car. He watched her run back along the road, and then kneel to the dirt. Minutes later she returned, breathing hard, a smile on her face.

"Onward," she said happily as she settled back into the passenger seat. "Beer?"

"Aren't you going to show me?"

"Nope."

"Wasn't really a collar, was it?"

She leaned between the seats, cleared the clutter from the top of the cooler, and came up with two cold beers. "Nope."

"Was it a car door, really?"

She handed him a beer and started to tuck the camera into its case. "Guess you'll never know."

"Come on. I stopped so you could get the picture."

"And?"

"And I'm sorry."

She held up the camera screen.

"Holy shit! That *is* a car door."

"Told you." She took a pull of her beer and smiled. "I love Baja."

Six hours later, they pulled into the village of San Evaristo. Roscoe was drunk and Tawny was driving. She drove through town and stopped beside the beach where they'd camped the day before. The afternoon breeze flicked white tongues at the chopping sea.

"We should walk the town and ask around," Roscoe slurred, stepping to the hot sand on bare feet.

Tawny unloaded two beach chairs and an umbrella. "Ask around?"

"See if anyone lost a bag of pearls." He patted his fanny pack lovingly where he kept the two small pearls.

"You want to wander around and ask strangers if they lost a bag of pearls?"

"Why not?"

"Because most of the townsfolk will think we're crazy. Everyone else will just say yes."

"I thought you liked the idea of finding the true owner." He slid the cooler of beer and ice from the backseat of the Land Rover and set it in the shade beneath the umbrella, then dropped heavily into a beach chair.

"I do."

"But?"

"But we don't know if the fisherman was from here or not." She sat beside him and fished a hand through the cooler. "It'll take some stealth to find our true owner." She raised a cold Negra Modelo from the ice, freed the Leatherman pliers strapped to her belt, unhinged its bottle opener, and popped the cap.

Roscoe lowered his sunglasses and watched her, the look in his bloodshot eyes curious.

Tawny took a satisfying gulp of the dark beer and said, "If you discovered an oyster bed that produced gorgeous pearls, and then you lost those pearls, what would you do?"

Roscoe slid the sunglasses back into place. He ran his fingers through his hair and smiled. "I'd return to the scene of the discovery."

Tawny raised her bottle in a toast. "Bingo."

CHAPTER TWENTY-ONE

Cabo San Lucas, Baja California Sur

The *Fish Goddess* rounded the famous arch rock near midnight and pulled into Cabo San Lucas Bay like a craft under attack. Two cruise ships were leaving and two were dropping anchor. The requisite wakeboarders and water-skiers, usually limited to daylight hours, shot beams of headlights across the water, their drivers playing drunken chicken with platoons of reckless Jet Skiers and Sea-Dooers. Yachts the size of clone homes were stacked three deep along Médano Beach, where swarms of partyers gyrated to dueling sound systems under the glare of portable sodium lights.

"Must be a holiday," Fish commented.

Skegs shrugged. "If it ends in a *y*, it's a holiday in Cabo. This is just the newest Chamber of Commerce promo. 'Cabo after Dark' they're calling it. I hope to God it's temporary."

Overhead, Fish and Skegs watched a middle-aged parasailer with a red face and a beer belly haloed by a powerful spotlight circle one of the anchored cruise ships where a crowd of passengers stood waiting for the tenders to take them to shore. The speedboat operator slowed just as the man passed over the crowd. He dropped his shorts, exposing a set of chalky white buttocks. The crowd cheered. The speedboat operator gunned the engines just as the man bent forward to retrieve his swim trunks, cinching the harness around his protruding gut and launching a copious plume of vomit into the well-lit night. Undigested carne asada tacos and a bellyful of Pacificos caught the light breeze and rained down on the horrified passengers.

"That's a first," Fish said, guiding the trawler along the lighted entrance to the marina.

"Disgusting," Skegs said, turning away.

"Your hour starts the minute we tie up to the dock."

"Roger that," Skegs said. "I called ahead. My man's meeting us at the dock with a truck." Skegs's jaw dropped then at the sight of an immense, glow-in-the-dark hot air balloon floating into position at the entrance to the marina. Below the basket hung an enormous green frog holding a guitar with the words *Señor Frog's* in lights across its chest.

Fish scowled.

Skegs made a note to hit up the manager for a few cases of his mescal.

Fish pulled back the throttles and entered the relative calm of the marina. He ran the gauntlet of dinghies, tipsy kayakers, and bikinied paddleboarders, and then pulled up to the busy public dock. Throngs of sunburned couples filled the patios of the bars and restaurants that lined the docks. The most popular by far was the restaurant with the overblown cartoon balloon of a happy green frog, where waiters in green sombreros filled shot glasses with abandon.

"Looks like the hot-air-balloon gimmick is working," Fish said without emotion.

"Maybe you should get a few for Mag Bay." Skegs tied the stern off to the nearest cleat. As he tightened the figure eight, a Mexican man pushing a dolly loaded with a case of Tecates approached and exchanged pleasantries with Skegs in rapid-fire Spanish. Fish eavesdropped and was soon opening the shark cage.

"Listo," he said when he'd finished, causing the two men to look up from their conversation.

"Sorry," Skegs said, and introduced his part-time employee. "Pedro, meet Atticus Fish. Fish, this is Pedro."

"Mucho gusto, amigo," Pedro said, and shook Fish's hand.

"Igualmente," Fish said.

The three amigos quickly loaded the dolly with ten cases of Macho Mescal, and Pedro wheeled it away.

After Skegs transferred the case of Tecates to the back-deck refrigerator, he opened one and said, "Ten trips at five minutes a trip and we're motoring. Pedro's got orders from every bar on the wharf."

Thirty minutes later, and only halfway through their offload, a group of college-aged men wearing togas exited Señor Frog's, spotted the trawler, and wandered up to its stern.

"Is that a shark cage?" one of the men slurred.

"What's under the tarp?" another asked.

"Is that shit any good?" came a third inquiry from a red-eyed man who was pointing at the remaining cases of mescal sitting inside the cage.

A similarly clad group of college-aged women stumbled from the bar and joined the men.

"Oooh, private booze cruise," the lead woman cried, and straddled the stern. "Come on, girls!" she hollered with an exaggerated wave, when a look of fear overtook her face.

The boat engine had come to life, and exhaust was billowing up around her toga. One of the men yelled. Fish hollered to Skegs, who hopped to the dock, deftly unwound the dock line from its cleat, and hopped back aboard. The engines revved and the boat shot forward, dropping the young woman into the dirty water.

Expletives filled the air. Threats and middle fingers followed. An empty beer bottle whizzed by Skegs's ear and exploded across the deck. Fish upped their speed, and minutes later they were planing across the bay toward open ocean.

"Dude," Skegs complained, "I still have twenty-five cases aboard."

"That was not going to end well."

"But—"

"We're stopping in La Paz. You can unload the rest there."

"We're stopping in La Paz?"

"Got some business to attend to."

"Some of my favorite clients are in La Paz."

"I know."

"And, dude, kudos on keeping it together back there. Other than the woman in the water thing. But there was a time you'd have gone all Bruce Lee, scare-you-with-my-machete on those drunks. For once you didn't turn into that crazy reckless guy and take on the whole gang of idiots."

"They were harmless," Fish said. "And maybe you're a good influence on me," he added with a doubtful tone.

"Damn straight I am."

That earned a half smile from Fish as he angled away from a tender filled with fresh tourists eager to leave the cruise ship and join the parties in town. "This place is a twenty-four-hour madhouse."

"Just when you think it can't get any worse, it doubles down on you."

"What do you say we take it slow and try a little nighttime swordfishing at the Gordo Banks?"

Skegs clapped his friend happily on the back. "You sure know how to make a guy feel good about losing—well, postponing—half his sales."

CHAPTER TWENTY-TWO

La Paz, Baja California Sur

After failing to raise a swordfish from the once-prolific Gordo Banks fishing grounds off San Jose del Cabo, Fish drove straight through the night, making better time than expected and pulling into Bahía de La Paz a little before dawn. Skegs took the wheel as the expatriate switched out the custom filters that allowed the trawler to run on fish oil and readied the diesel tank for its five hundred gallons of new fuel. By the time he'd finished, the morning had broken calm and clear with a man-o'-war sky and an equally blue bay bursting with sea life.

Flying fish took to the sky like castoffs, their glistening wings spread wide, their tails flicking the surface as fast as propellers. Frigate birds circled high overhead, plummeting like aerobatic airplanes and then pulling up at the final second to snatch the winged fish in their long-hooked bills. Pelicans molested schools of rising sardines. Small pods of dolphins carved arcs of white water in pursuit of the juvenile skipjack tuna and schooling *caballitos*. A sea turtle lazed in the early-morning sun.

Skegs pulled the *Fish Goddess* up to the fuel dock and waited as Fish secured the cleat lines.

"Huevos a la Mexicana?" Skegs asked after Fish finished flemishing the lines. "The breakfast at the Dock Café is almost as good as Mamacita's."

"She used to work here years ago."

"That explains it."

"I need to call my attorney and set up a quick meeting this morning," Fish said, ducking into the saloon for a shower and a change of clothes. He emerged ten minutes later in a fresh pair of sailcloth pants, a Guayabera shirt, and a new fish-skin cap fashioned from the hides of a recent catch of corvina that had swarmed the shores of his beachfront sand dune. Even without shoes Fish towered above Skegs, who descended the helm stairs after changing into a blue AFTCO fishing shirt covered in game fish, and a pair of tan board shorts. He wore huaraches and a pair of expensive polarized sunglasses.

"Was checking out the boats while you were wasting money on a lawyer and getting pretty," he said as they each stepped to the dock and headed toward the restaurant.

"Armando's worth every peso," Fish said. "Especially with his political connections. And yes, there's a nice steel-hulled DeFever on the other side of the marina."

"I'm interested in the one over there." Skegs pointed.

"*The Grand Banks*?"

"Naw, man. The little cruiser next to it with the advertisement."

Fish squinted. "*Reel Cool*?"

"Was thinking about this pearling thing you're dragging me out on."

Fish waited.

"You get to do all the cool stuff—flying a fat-ass plane, cruising around in a submarine—while I have to sit around bored out of my mind."

"You get to fish."

"Finding a few pearls sounds more lucrative."

"We're only talking a few pearls."

Skegs gave him a surprised look. "You were *serious* about that extinction bullshit? Come on, man. We aren't talking beaches or islands or big beautiful dodos for the barbeque. These are oysters. Ugly barnacle-covered slimy things that stick to rocks. Hell, man, nobody ever sees them. Good for nothing but cocktail sauce and making pearls. Pearls for us."

Fish stopped walking and tugged thoughtfully at his braided goatee. "Why are we friends again?"

"'Cause you need my knowledge when it comes to everything cool. Like finding pearls."

"Uh-huh."

"How about I take just enough oysters to make one necklace?"

"How about I leave you on the dock?"

"One pearl?"

"No."

"Fine," he said stubbornly. "But I'm still diving."

"Hope you can swim fast."

Skegs started for the restaurant. "Yeah, whatever."

"You really thinking about renting a scuba-diving boat?"

"Hell no. Just enough gear to canvas the whole damn island. We'll see who finds the pearls first."

"Oysters," Fish corrected him.

Skegs shook his head in irritation.

They reached the dock gate and Fish paused. "I didn't know you were licensed to dive."

"There you go again with the details. This is Baja, man. No need for a license."

"People die scuba diving."

"People die walking across the street."

"Reckless talk."

Skegs choked down a laugh. "Now *you're* going to lecture *me* about recklessness? Mister I-think-I'll-take-on-three-UFC-dudes-at-once guy? And that's just the beginning." He turned to look at his friend. "Should we discuss bullet wounds?"

Fish shrugged.

"Then, it's settled. You're buying breakfast, meeting with your lawyer to play God or whatever it is you lawyers do, while I go pawn off ten more cases of damn good hooch, get a few scuba tanks and whatever else I need to out-pearl your sorry ass."

Fish agreed with the wink of an eye and followed Skegs into the restaurant.

After breakfast, Fish called his attorney and left a message, then hailed a taxi to the grocery store for a week's worth of supplies. Skegs, meanwhile, wandered back to the slip where the owner of the *Reel Cool* sat on the back deck drinking his breakfast from a twelve-ounce can.

"Can I help you?" he asked Skegs, who'd stopped at the transom.

"I'd like to rent some scuba gear."

"Ain't got none."

Skegs glanced up at the banner tied between the outriggers. "Says you're a dive boat."

"And a fishing boat, if the idea suits you."

"Got any fishing gear on board?"

"Most anything you want."

"But not any scuba gear?" Skegs asked suspiciously.

"Scuba's a new venture for me. Gonna have to see my partner to get the gear."

"He around?"

The old man finished his beer and opened another. "You ever dived before?"

"Sure," Skegs lied.

"Don't matter to us. Just need to breathe. That way your lungs don't explode on the way up."

"I'll remember that." Skegs looked around at the disheveled dock. "About your partner. Where can I find him?"

"'Bout a quarter mile from here. Few blocks in from the *malecón*. Place called Diving Dudes. Any cabbie can get you there. Or you can walk. Not too hot yet."

"Much obliged." Skegs turned to go.

The old man tossed his empty beer can into a bucket draped with dried fish guts, and Skegs heard him pop the top on the next as he walked away. "He's got mismatched eyes," he called after him with a wet cough.

Skegs turned. "Say again?"

"Feller's eyes are different colors. Just thought I'd warn you."

Skegs thanked the man. He commissioned a dock cart from the collection area near the gate and returned to the *Fish Goddess*. Thirty minutes after loading the cart with the remaining cases of mescal, he was staring through the grimy glass door of the Diving Dudes.

Skegs parked the cart of mescal in a shaded piece of sidewalk and ducked inside the shop, unaware of the broken-down Winnebago parked up the street beneath an enormous jacaranda tree, its purple flowers brilliant in the morning sun.

"Wake up!" Tank yelled at Jimbo, who was slouched in the passenger seat, snoring loudly. In the back, Mikey stirred at the sound of the bigger man's growl.

The three UFC hopefuls had parked the Winnebago up the street from Diving Dudes after meeting the owner in a run-down bar the night before. They'd left a voice mail with the pale-skinned Canadian that they'd arranged for a week's worth of tanks and gear from a shifty American dude with two-toned eyes named Kraken. Obviously on the lam, and as crooked as they come.

Crooked and drunk.

He'd come to their attention when they'd overheard him talking to another expatriate about a couple he'd taken scuba diving earlier in the day. How the woman refused to go into the water once they were on the seamount. How the blowhard boyfriend hyperventilated at the first sight of a shark and nearly drowned. How the woman threatened to sue. How Kraken backed her into the stern rail as the boyfriend vomited ham and cheese over the bow. Backed her into the stern rail and directed his partner, their drunk captain, to commandeer her purse from the saloon.

Then with a honky-tonk flourish, Kraken had slapped the woman's driver's license to the bar.

"Told the bitch she cause me any problems, I use her license here to notify my stateside felon buds to pay her and her loser boyfriend a visit. Thought she was gonna vomit, too." He choked out a boozy laugh and pocketed the license.

Tank immediately bought the man a beer. Thirty minutes later Kraken had agreed to front them scuba tanks and dive gear and a portable compressor for half his usual price. No dive licenses required, no paperwork signed. Nada. All they had to do was stop by the dive shop in the morning with some cold hard American *dinero*.

"I said wake the fuck up!" Tank barked again, ignoring the sting of sweat covering his infected head.

"Huh?" Mikey responded groggily. He rubbed his face and winced at the touch of the fresh scabs lining his patchy sideburns. Three long, thin furrows that exactly matched the claws of the iguana that had clung to his face two days before. Mikey had almost forgotten about the expatriate's bar he'd reluctantly watched his unstable cohorts burn down—until he felt the scratches.

Tank punched the steering wheel and glared back at Mikey with eyes like radishes and a scalp boiling with infection. "The fucking Indian who tried to drown us," he spat.

"What about him?" Jimbo muttered from the passenger seat, where he'd passed out after midnight. His homemade arm sling stunk of stale beer, and his mouth was as dry as beach sand.

Tank peered through the cracked windshield. "Motherfucker's going into the dive shop."

Jimbo bolted upright, then blanched at the sudden throbbing in his head. "He's what?"

Tank jabbed a finger. "The dive shop. Two seconds ago. He was pushing a goddamn cart like some homeless guy."

"Dive shop's open already?" Mikey asked with a yawn.

Tank punched the steering wheel again. "He walked right in, so yeah, I'd say it's open, you idiot!"

"Let's go fuck him up," Jimbo said, massaging his temples. "Kicking the shit out of somebody's exactly what I need this morning."

Mikey stood up. "What I need is food. I'm hungry."

Tank whirled around and fixed a withering glare on the younger man. "Are you fucking deaf, Mikey? Tonto just walked into our dive shop."

Mikey shrugged. "He was pretty good with that net. Maybe we should leave him alone."

Tank blinked as though he didn't understand, his bloodshot eyes pulsing.

"I mean," Mikey stuttered, "that maybe he and the dive shop guy know each other. Maybe he's here to rent some gear."

"Then we'll fuck 'em both up," Jimbo snarled.

"But—"

"But nothing, Mikey," Jimbo said, opening the passenger door. "Three against two. Gonna be a bad day for the dive shop guy if he's with the Indian."

Tank grabbed his friend by the back of the shirt. "I've got a better idea."

"Better than beating the shit out of that fuckwad? He tried to *drown* us, man. We gotta make him pay."

"Ten grand better."

Jimbo closed the car door. "How are we going to get ten grand for beating up a dumb Indian?"

"Ransom," Tank announced proudly, wiping sweat from his eyes. "The Injun's butt buddy who owns the bar we torched has to be rich if he also owns that big-ass boat with the shark cage."

"I don't know," Mikey said. "Rich guys know people. Like cops and judges."

Tank spun again. "You're starting to piss me off, Mikey. No white guy's going to go and complain to the Mexicans. Not if he wants his buddy back alive."

"But the dive shop owner," Mikey said. "He might not like us kidnapping one of his customers."

Tank's infected head reddened further as he contemplated and dismissed this possibility. "Were you not in the same bar as us last night? The diving dude's as dirty as they get. He'll probably want in on the action."

Mikey cleared his throat. "The Canadian guy said to find a dive shop owner who could keep a secret. He didn't say anything about kidnapping."

"He didn't offer us no ten grand, either," Jimbo cracked. He reached behind his seat and fished a can of beer from a broken Styrofoam cooler.

"That's what I'm talking about!" Tank said, a beaming smile showcasing his missing tooth.

"The Indian won't go down without a fight," Mikey reminded them.

Tank reached under his seat and freed a rusty tire iron. "Perfect. We're hardly getting any training in at all."

Skegs took a moment to allow his eyes to adjust to the dimness of the dive shop. The one-room business was sparsely stocked with a few scuba tanks, some old masks and snorkels, and a clouded glass counter near the back corner covered in dust. A rusty speargun rested upright against the counter. Skegs was about to leave, when a squat man with stringy black hair, a scarred face, and mismatched eyes stood from the gloom behind the glass counter.

"Looking for a dive?" the man asked, squinting at him.

"Didn't mean to wake you," Skegs said. He motioned toward the front. "Door was unlocked."

The freakish man yawned. "Forgot to lock it last night."

"You live here?"

"It's my shop," the man said matter-of-factly, combing his few black filaments from his face. "Kraken."

Skegs blinked at him. "Sorry?"

"My name," the man said. "Kraken. What do you need?"

"I was hoping to rent some gear for a week or so."

"Got a boat?"

Skegs nodded.

"You ever dived before?"

"Sure," Skegs lied.

"How many dives you planning on?"

"Not sure." Skegs glanced around again. "How many tanks you got?"

"Half dozen filled." He walked out from behind the counter. "You want I can scrounge a portable compressor. Extra hundred for the week."

"And the gear?"

"Makes it—"

The front door burst open, and three muscle-bound men charged inside. The lead man's shaved head was misshapen and glistening with oily sweat. He carried a rusty tire iron.

"Hands up, motherfuckers!" Tank hollered, waving the tire iron above his head. Jimbo pounced on Skegs and wrestled him to the ground. Mikey lagged behind watchfully.

"You boys picked a piss-poor place to rob," Kraken said, inching back toward the speargun. "And besides, after last night, I thought we were friends."

Tank caught his movement toward the speargun and lunged. The tire iron shattered the glass counter, sending the speargun clattering across the floor.

Kraken froze, his discolored eyes flat.

"You got a choice, mister," Tank said to him, then glanced down at Jimbo and Mikey, who had reluctantly helped Jimbo hog-tie and gag Skegs. He looked back at Kraken. "You can thank your lucky stars this ain't really a holdup. You can forget you ever saw us, or you can play hero and get the worst beating of your miserable life." He showed a wide, gap-toothed grin. "Don't make no difference to us."

Kraken held up his hands. "I'm cool with the first option."

Tank retrieved the speargun from the broken glass and let it hang loose in his left hand. Keeping a tight grip on the tire iron in his right, he turned to his accomplices. "Stand him up, Jimbo. Mikey, go get the Winnebago and drive it up here fast. Make sure the side door opens parallel with the front door. Don't need no strangers watching us haul out this trash." He laughed at his joke, then turned to flash Kraken another gap-toothed grin. "The gear we talked about last night, I want you to load it into the Winnebago."

"I thought you said this wasn't a holdup."

"It ain't."

Kraken narrowed his one bleached eye.

Tank raised the speargun. "Hundred bucks for the use of the gear and the loss of your memory."

Kraken didn't answer.

"I'll take that as a yes."

"Speargun's loaded," Kraken said coldly. "Could you point it somewhere else?"

"The Canadian guy we told you about is going to pay us. When he does, we'll give you your share."

"Funny way to start a partnership," Kraken said, motioning the spear away from his chest.

Jimbo shoved Skegs into Mikey's arms and took a lunging step toward Kraken, who didn't flinch. "We work alone, asshole," Jimbo told him.

Kraken pursed his lips and nodded. "Except if you're kidnapping this dude or even just taking him somewhere to whack him, you're going to need a place to stow him, alive or dead. And a faster way out of Baja than an old Winnebago. There's only one road north. You'll be sitting ducks without my help."

Jimbo turned to Tank, who blinked away a trickle of pus and sweat from his forehead as he considered what Kraken had said. He liked the idea of a hideaway. He was also tired of the Winnebago and its sour-smelling seats and misfiring engine. He closed his eyes and tried to concentrate through the mounting fever. The cockeyed dude might be useful.

He opened his eyes. "What kind of faster ride we talking about?"

This time Kraken smiled. "My business partner's cooling off in Montana for the summer," he lied. "I'm watching his apartment for him. A place with a classic Buick in the garage." Both eyes narrowed beguilingly. "Eight cylinders. No traceable plates."

Tank lowered the speargun. He turned to Skegs and cocked the tire iron above one of his shoulders. "Step away from him, Mikey."

"He's secure, Tank. No need to hurt him."

"The Winnebago!" Tank ordered. "Get it. Now!"

Mikey hesitated and then hurried to the front door. As he stepped into the sunlight, he glanced back just as Tank swung the iron.

CHAPTER TWENTY-THREE

Isla San Jose, Baja California Sur

The sky broke almost colorless as Zaragosa woke Manolín. They'd left the village of San Evaristo before dawn and arrived in darkness, anchoring just outside an enormous sea cave with thirty-foot ceilings and slick walls decorated in streaks of rose-colored strata. Zaragosa knew the cave well. His forefathers performed rituals in its rocky womb, beseeching the generosity of the sea-gods and invoking deities no longer esteemed. It was a tradition passed down from father to son and eventually to Zaragosa himself as a young man gifted with frigate bird vision and reflexes rivaling the strike of a sidewinder.

But that was long ago. Before the tourists descended in great white clouds, spending pesos as though money was unimportant, an afterthought for the wealthy gringos dropping American dollars into every outstretched hand. As carefree as the white-winged gulls wheeling in the dry Baja winds. It was easy to covet such generosity. To want a better life than hauling fish into a *panga*. It was a sentiment Zaragosa's son held, along with many of his generation. He was a boy who yearned for the sins of *El Norte*. A son who rejected tradition. A man who abandoned family and country. A stranger no one had heard from since.

"It is time," Zaragosa whispered to the young boy, who had curled up tightly in a woolen blanket just beneath the bow.

Manolín buried himself deeper inside the blanket.

Zaragosa gently shook his shoulders. "The sea is waking, *Nieto*. We must wake with it."

Manolín opened his eyes. It took a moment to remember where he was, but the sway of the *panga* and the lapping of the current against the hull pulled him from his dreams.

"*Abuelo,*" he said happily, his young eyes immediately bright and alert. He sat up and hugged his grandfather. "How is your arm?"

"Better," the old man said. "*Listo?*"

"*Sí.*"

Manolín folded the blanket into a square and tucked it beneath the middle thwart. Then he grasped the anchor rope and hauled up the small grapnel.

Zaragosa primed the outboard and was soon speeding toward the reef where days before he'd discovered riches beyond his dreams. A bed of oysters untouched since the days of the Yacqui Indians and their loincloths and sharpened palo verde branches used to pry the shells from the undersea rocks. Oysters that bred the rare teardrop pearl. The occasional purple-hued gems of great value.

Oysters capable of clouding an old man's reason. Never again, Zaragosa reminded himself as they neared the reef.

He spotted the barely discernible discoloration beneath the surface and slowed the *panga*.

"*Allá,*" he called out, and motioned to Manolín.

Manolín readied the anchor.

Zaragosa circled the reef once and then said, "*Listo.*"

Manolín swung the anchor overboard. He waited for it to hit bottom and then allowed the light current to take out enough line to set a three-to-one scope. Zaragosa nodded approvingly as he watched the boy tie the rope to the bow cleat. He reached into the hatch beneath his seat and tossed Manolín the mask and snorkel the *mecánico* had given him as a gift after Zaragosa had mentioned his plans to salvage what he had lost when his boat capsized. A new mask and snorkel with a clear faceplate and seams that didn't leak. Proper flippers like the ones the gringos were so fond of using.

Sized just right for Manolín. Carlos had even added a second set of everything for Zaragosa when his arm healed.

"I am ready, *Papi*," Manolín said.

Zaragosa crossed himself and said a prayer.

Manolín waited for him to finish, then splashed over the side of the *panga* and stared through the mask at a reef twenty feet below him. Colorful fish darted among the rocks. Sea fans swayed with the current. A moray eel poked its head from beneath a boulder and carped its green mouth menacingly.

Manolín sucked in a deep breath and kicked for the bottom. At first the buoyancy of his lungs pulled against him and he was thankful for the flippers, which he kicked hard to drive him deeper. The pressure tightened the mask against his face, and his ears began to ache. He pinched his nose and blew air against his nostrils as his grandfather taught him when diving for *caracoles* off the beach of his village. All at once, the depth equalized his buoyancy, and he settled gently to the reef.

He stared wide-eyed at his surroundings. He'd never worn such a clear mask, and for the fist time in his young life the world beneath the waves came alive like a dream. He reached for a mango-sized blowfish hiding in the reef, its tiny fins vibrating, its bulbous eyes watchful. Manolín caught the slow-moving fish in his palms and gently squeezed, waiting as it puffed up like a coconut, revealing a hide of sharp spines. Manolín laughed out bubbles of air and released the spiny ball, watching it slowly deflate and swim back to the safety of the rocks.

Manolín felt his chest burn from the lack of oxygen and looked up at the surface with its shimmering shafts of sunlight. He glanced back at the reef and remembered the oysters. He turned and kicked for the sunlight.

"*Papi! Papi!*" he cried out as he broke the surface. "The water is so clear and the fish are unafraid."

"The oysters, did you find them?" Zaragosa asked.

Manolín frowned. "I am sorry. There was so much to see. But I will find them now. I promise."

"*Vaya con Dios,*" the old man said.

Manolín took a full breath and angled toward a flat stretch of reef. He leveled out just above the sea fans and urchins and tubeworms, and began searching for the large hunchbacked shells. Soon his lungs burned. He ignored the pain in his chest and kicked his legs, propelling himself along the reef. In the distance he spotted an oyster clinging to a rock, its shell parted slightly, wisps of seaweed fluttering around the opening. He swam hard to it and saw more of the large crustaceans clinging to the rocks.

Manolín's heart raced.

He grasped the nearest oyster in both hands and wrenched upward. Nothing. He pulled again, his vision clouding, his chest on fire. He yanked harder, but the oyster remained glued to the rock. Hot tears fell from his eyes, fogging his mask. He screamed into the water and hauled back with an explosive kick of the flippers and felt the oyster release. He sprang upward, thrashing his legs and feet, lungs begging for oxygen. He broke the surface like a breaching seal, tearing the mask from his face with great gulps of air.

"*Mira!*" he screamed when his breath returned. "I found one!" He held up the oyster and took another series of breaths. "The reef is full of them. Hundreds, maybe thousands. They go deeper and deeper, *Papi.* We are rich!" He swam to the *panga* and dropped the oyster inside. "Open it. See if it has a pearl inside."

Zaragosa wagged his gray head dolefully. "A pearl is a blessing. Only the most special oysters carry one. We must collect dozens more to find even one."

"Maybe this one is blessed."

"Maybe."

"Open it," he insisted.

Zaragosa unsheathed the knife and split the seam. His eyes held hope as the blade pierced the innards and the shell popped open, but then his face dropped. "You did good, *Nieto*," he said with a gentle smile, "but this one is blessed only for the dinner table."

Manolín shrugged. "I will fill the *panga, Papi.* I can swim all day." His eyes were wide with excitement behind the faceplate. "And all night."

Zaragosa shook his head. "Greed is *el diablo,* Manolín. We will harvest a small bagful each day and return to our village each night. We must avoid the curiosity of the others."

"*Sí,*" Manolín agreed. "We can search for oysters *and* fish."

"Come. Take a short break and drink water." Zaragosa reached over the gunwale with his good arm and pulled Manolín into the boat. "You have school to think of."

Manolín looked away. "But I want to be with you."

"Yes. And I need you with me. But school is important for a boy your age. We will take only a small break from your studies. Until my arm heals."

Manolín hugged his grandfather. "*Gracias, Papi!* I promise I will return to school when we have found all the pearls."

Zaragosa's old face lifted. "*Te amo mucho,*" he said gratefully. He looked toward the island where the land had crumbled so recently and the sea had nearly swallowed him, and he crossed himself again.

"Another oyster?" he asked, his voice bridled with emotion as he reached out and handed Manolín the shucking blade. "I forgot to give you this. It will make the harvesting much easier."

Manolín took the knife with a happy shriek and leaped overboard.

CHAPTER TWENTY-FOUR

La Paz, Baja California Sur

By late morning, Atticus Fish was annoyed. It had been three hours since Skegs veered off in search of diving gear. Gear and a promised quick stop at a favorite tourist hangout to unload the remaining cases of mescal. Stella's was La Paz's well-known watering hole with its beautiful bartenders and affable manager. Fish had warned his friend to avoid the small talk and the invariable free drinks. The *Fish Goddess* was set to sail at ten o'clock sharp.

"Ten minutes flirting with the barkeep," Skegs had promised. "Five minutes with the owner to collect ten large ones and I'm out of there."

That had been two hours ago.

Now, as Fish trudged along the *malecón* in the breaching sun, he found himself cursing his friend. The anger from the loss of his bar had bubbled back to the top with the mescal salesman's inconsiderate behavior. It was totally out of character for Skegs to go on a morning bender with the *Fish Goddess* ready to shove off. Especially after Fish had allowed him to stop to fish not once but twice en route to La Paz.

Fish was thinking about what he would say to his friend when, in the distance, he spotted the weekend crowd spilling onto the sidewalk across from the *malecón*. He upped his pace, tugging absently at his braided goatee. He was barefoot as usual and wore a wide-brimmed fish-skin cap to shade his whiskered face from the sun.

Skegs had always been quick to criticize the expatriate's recklessness, and Fish couldn't argue the point. How could he? A lawyer's emotions were reactionary. Fight rather than flight. But survival instincts had kept him alive. The ones who'd died had been bent on destroying him and the ones he loved. *They* were reckless.

Still, Fish knew, it was his own aggressiveness in protecting his friends that had contributed to those deaths. Unplanned killings that bothered him late at night when sleep was impossible. First, it was the *Wahoo Rhapsody* and drug dealers intent on stealing the boat and destroying his business partner and the men who worked for him. Then it was the happy-go-lucky archaeologist and the hit men intent on murder in order to possess the infamous Jesuit Treasure. Fish hadn't planned on killing any of them. He'd been content to live quietly on his island paradise. But as with all things precious, justice comes in many forms, and when the innocent are bullied, caution becomes a casualty. He had reacted in order to protect.

And Skegs had always been at his side. Willing and loyal, and mostly helpful. But the man was also gregarious and lovable, adept at drawing strangers into his life. A gift possessed by hustlers and snake-oil salesmen, and the most successful mescal bootlegger in Baja. Fish had recognized it from their first meeting, when the lanky Indian sold him a trunkful of homemade mescal and fake ironwood.

He'd also recognized the demons they had in common. The drunken devil with a foolish glaze to the eye. The Indian's binges sometimes led to heated love affairs; other times to unplanned excursions at a drug lord's mainland hideaway or a topless dancer's Cabo San Lucas cathouse. Once the mescal salesman even joined a crew of yachties fueling in Cabo for a week of fishing the *revillagigedos* for yellowfin tuna and wahoo. All it took was some free mescal and that winning smile.

But the circumstances on this morning felt different somehow. Skegs knew the importance of getting to the oyster grounds. Fish had compromised more than once since leaving Magdalena Bay. It was one thing for his friend to take advantage of a generous partyer at a tourist-filled happy hour when their work was done and their plans flexible. But this was neither happy hour nor flexible. As he entered the bar, Fish felt his anger rise at his friend's indifference. Music blasted. Tourists sang and drank. Fish scanned the throng of midday partyers and approached the bar.

"Soda, please."

"Straight?" the Mexican bartender asked. She wore a pair of skin-tight jeans and a torn T-shirt covered in cartoon sharks.

Fish nodded. He watched the drinkers sing and dance to the overplayed song. "Macarena" was timeless down in Baja. Same tune, same party, different setting. He looked through the crowd again, and saw no sign of Skegs. He sighed impatiently.

The bartender set his Coke to the bar. "Three bucks."

Fish handed her a twenty. "A friend of mine sells mescal. I wonder—"

"Skegs!" she shouted gleefully. "Where is that handsome Indian? Tell him we need more of his *Macho*." She said the last word in a suggestive tone.

"You haven't seen him?"

"I wish," she said while taking an order from a sunburned couple for two strawberry margaritas. "You a friend of his?"

"And a customer. If you see him, please send someone to Marina de La Paz. I'm on a boat. The *Fish Goddess*. He and I were supposed to leave hours ago." He heard the concern in his voice. He reached into his pocket and handed her a hundred-dollar bill. "I'm Atticus."

"Unusual name." She took the money. "I'll keep a lookout. And don't be a stranger." She winked. "Cute goatee."

Fish felt his hand instinctively go to the metal crimp at the end of his chin braid. "Thanks," he said, trying to ignore the acidic worry rising in his stomach as he left the soda on the bar and raced outside.

He backtracked halfway to the marina, then turned inland and walked the three short blocks to where Skegs had said the dive shop was located. Diving Dudes. Fish found the shabby storefront with a Closed sign in the window. When he leaned to the glass door, cupped his hands to the sides of his face, and peered inside, he saw that the dark room was in shambles. Broken glass covered the floor where a display case had been smashed. A smattering of dive gear filled the dust-covered shelves, and the walls were bare but for peeling paint.

Fish felt his stomach tighten. He tried the door. Locked. He walked around the block and into the back alley and froze. Near the back door of the dive shop was the Marina de La Paz luggage cart Skegs had loaded with mescal. It was empty and broken and flipped onto its side.

Fish hurried to the alley door and turned the handle. It, too, was locked. He banged with his palm and felt its flimsiness. He glanced around the deserted alley, and then kicked the door in with the heel of a callused foot.

He cautiously entered the darkness, hoping Skegs wasn't sprawled out on the floor in a pool of blood. What he found was dust and neglect.

And a pool of blood.

"No," he muttered, and sprinted from the dive shop.

CHAPTER TWENTY-FIVE

La Paz, Baja California Sur

Tank glanced down at the prisoner duct-taped to their lawn chair in the back of the Winnebago and grinned. Skegs's left eye was swollen shut and his blue AFTCO game-fish shirt was wet with vomit from the repeated application of the tire iron to his midsection. Still, the Indian glared at his captors through his good eye.

"Think he might want a little more," Tank said.

"Bet you broke a rib," Jimbo bragged. "Emptied the fucker's stomach with those shots." He raised the bottle of Macho Mescal and took a long swig. "A fucking Jerry Maguire home run."

"Mark McGwire," Mikey corrected quietly.

Both Jimbo and Tank eyed the younger man with annoyance, Tank slapping the tire iron into his open palm. His scalp had worsened with the heat of the day and now resembled an enormous pox-covered pomegranate.

His attention shifting back to the bloody work Tank had made of Skegs, Jimbo got past Mikey's impudence in correcting him. "We should cut off his ear, man," he said. "Send it to the rich fucker. Bloody up the ransom note, too. Show the dude we're serious about this shit."

Mikey, who stood near the side door, flinched. The heat flushed his youthful features and highlighted the matching scratch marks on his cheeks. "I don't think we should do anything that permanent."

Jimbo turned on him. "He tried to fucking drown us, you pussy!"

"Still," Mikey mumbled, shying away from the bigger man, "we should be cautious until the dive shop guy calls about the hideaway."

Still smacking his palm with the iron, Tank began to pace the interior of the Winnebago. "He'll call. Good idea about the ear, but let's save that for if the rich guy refuses to pay."

"That's weak!" Jimbo sneered. "Guy's got two ears."

Tank swung the iron without warning, and the bottle of mescal exploded beneath Jimbo's hand.

"Fuck was that for!" Jimbo screeched, and dropped the neck of glass to the threadbare carpet. He moved to the Styrofoam cooler and buried his fingers into the icy water. "You could have broken my hand!"

"Watch. Your. Mouth."

"You could have just said it without busting a perfectly good bottle of tequila."

"Mescal," Skegs corrected flatly.

Jimbo jerked his head around and flung a handful of ice his way across the room. The frozen water sailed past Skegs and bounced off the peeling wallpaper.

"Um," Mikey said carefully, "shouldn't we write the ransom note?"

"You've got the best handwriting," Tank said. "Grab a pen and paper and lay out the terms."

"We don't have any."

Tank reached into the pocket of his sweat-soaked jeans and handed Mikey the stolen iPhone. "Fuck the note. When you get him on the phone, tell him we want ten grand or his buddy loses an ear."

"But we don't know his number."

Seeing the phone, Skegs laughed. "You idiots stole my cell phone but left my wallet behind? That was even dumber than burning down the bar."

Tank lunged at him and caught a handful of curly hair, nearly yanking Skegs and the chair from the floor. "What's his number?"

"I doubt he wants to talk to the assholes who torched his place," Skegs said, nearly choking on the smell of the man's breath.

"Crack his head open, Tank," Jimbo said, finishing the Modelo. He reached for another, then changed his mind and pulled an unopened bottle of Macho Mescal from one of the cases. "I'll give you redskins one thing. You sure know how to make good hooch."

Tank released the handful of hair, then set Skegs back on the floor and cocked the tire iron.

"Hey hey hey!" Mikey said, rushing across the room. "If you kill him, we'll never get the ten grand."

Mikey winced as Tank nearly swung the iron in his direction, but then Tank lowered it. He was wheezing slightly now and appeared confused.

"Finally someone with more than a thimbleful of brains," Skegs observed.

Jimbo slammed the mescal bottle onto a table. "What the fuck did he just say?"

Skegs's insult appeared to have focused Tank's dwindling faculties. "He said Mikey's smart and we're dumb." He took a batter's stance and aimed the tire iron at Skegs's kneecap.

"He's here in La Paz," Skegs blurted.

"That right?" Tank straightened.

"Bullshit," Jimbo said. "He's stalling to try and escape. Hit him!"

Skegs said, "We arrived this morning by boat. He's docked at Marina de La Paz."

Tank stomped down on Skegs's foot, tearing loose the leather straps of his huaraches. "You better not be lying, motherfucker." He tapped Skegs on the temple with the end of the tire iron. "Why would he come here when his bar just burned down?"

Blinking back the pain in his foot, Skegs said, "To hunt down three bags of coyote piss."

Mikey's jaw dropped open.

Tank stepped back and began to laugh, slowly at first; then he burst into a roaring fit of laughter followed by a chest-rattling cough. He sank to the swaybacked couch and wiped a river of pus from his forehead. "This guy's got the biggest balls in Baja," he panted.

Jimbo charged across the room and knocked Skegs to the floor, but before he could land a blow, Mikey had him in a full nelson.

"'Bout time you showed some fight, Mikey," Tank said. He reluctantly stood and pulled the two men from Skegs. "Settle down, Jimbo, and let me finish this." He reset Skegs's chair to the center of the room, leaned close to his face, and said, "Why the fuck are you and this Fish asshole here in La Paz?"

Skegs turned his face away from the man's rancid odor and said, "He needs to hire workers to rebuild the bar. La Paz has the best palapa builders in Baja."

Tank hooked an index finger into Skegs's cheek and turned his face. "Does he think we did the bar?"

"What do you think, Einstein?"

Tank clasped Skegs's throat with a sweaty palm and squeezed. "Where's the boat? Exactly?"

"Fuel dock," Skegs croaked. "He won't leave without me."

Jimbo shook loose of Mikey's arm lock and said, "Why should we believe some good-for-nothing Indian?"

"Because I make good mescal."

Tank laughed again.

Jimbo gave a reluctant snort of approval and retrieved the bottle of mescal. He leaned on the arm of the passenger seat and took a slug.

Tank turned to Mikey. "Check the contacts for a guy named Fish."

"It's under Atticus," Skegs informed them.

"He's right," Mikey said, holding out the phone. "Here it is."

"Call him," Tank said.

Jimbo belched and stared at Mikey. "Try not to fuck it up. And next time you touch me, you're dead."

"I can't do it with everyone glaring at me," Mikey said. "Plus our guest might start yelling out information."

"Do it outside then," Tank said.

Mikey opened the Winnebago's side door, squinting as he stepped out into the flood of sunlight.

"Hey," Jimbo yelled after him. Mikey ducked his head back inside. "Don't even think about leading the rich guy back here."

"Why the hell would I do that, Jimbo? Might as well turn myself into the cops."

"For all we know, you're thinking of that, too. You seem damn worried about this guy's health. Just know that if you go soft on us, you won't like what happens to you."

Tank cleared his throat. "And get me some bottled water. I'm burning up inside this sardine can."

"Okay," Mikey said. "But you haven't told me where we want him to drop the money."

"You're going to meet him and bring it back here personally."

"Meet him?" Mikey stuttered. "Why me?"

"'Cause I'm tired and Jimbo's too drunk."

"I ain't drunk," Jimbo protested.

"And because I know you won't double-cross us."

Jimbo slammed down his beer. "How the fuck can you be so sure, Tank? Fucking little squid threw down on me a few minutes ago, and I never thought he'd do that, either."

"Because," Tank said, turning his bilious eyes on Mikey, "he tries to double-cross us, we'll carve up the Indian and spread his parts all over this shithole of a town."

Mikey swallowed dryly.

Showing his gap-toothed grin and smacking the tire iron into his palm, Tank stared hard at Mikey. "And then we'll come looking for *him*."

CHAPTER TWENTY-SIX

Isla San Jose, Baja California Sur

After a quick lunch of burritos packed the night before by their *mecánico* benefactor, Manolín was back in the water. He'd harvested thirty oysters, and not one contained a pearl. Zaragosa kept suggesting they head back home, but Manolín's youthful optimism kept them on the reef. The sun shone brightly, and a breeze had risen with the afternoon sun. Small whitecaps frayed the beryl sea.

Manolín surfaced suddenly. "I found another big one, *Papi!*" he sputtered, yanking the snorkel from his mouth. "I almost have it." He took a fast breath and disappeared just as a pair of frigate birds dropped from a rocky precipice on the island, their black feathers stark against the turquoise sky.

Zaragosa cradled his broken arm and said his prayer again. He no longer believed it would bring the boy luck with the pearls, but he said it with the same heartfelt emotion so as not to anger the sea. A burst of exhaled air caught his attention, and he turned away from where Manolín dived toward the open ocean and saw the footprint of a juvenile finback whale. Moments later a larger whale surfaced, and a great burst of air echoed across the water. Zaragosa smiled. Life had moved so fast lately, he'd forgotten the permanence of the sea. Her welcoming persistence. Her mostly predictable moods.

"*Papi!*" Manolín hollered happily as he broke the surface, snapping Zaragosa out of his musings. "I have two this time. Both are big ones! Heavier than the others. Maybe these will change our luck."

"*Posible*," Zaragosa agreed, his spirits lifted doubly by the whales and the boy's enthusiasm.

Manolín rolled to his back like an otter and kicked to the boat. He passed the oysters to his grandfather, who set the oysters to the center thwart and helped the boy aboard.

Yanking the mask from his face with one hand, Manolín pointed at the larger of the two large oysters with the other. "That one first, *Papi!*"

Zaragosa slid the shucking blade between the rough shells and twisted. The shells resisted. He moved the blade along the pleat and torqued the handle of the knife. The oyster opened, and the sun reflected only the slick gray meat, with its tendrils of muscle and strings of pale mucus. The old man tossed it to the bucket with the others.

"Tomorrow is a new day," he said to the boy. "Sunday. *El día de Dios.* Maybe a luckier day, no?"

Manolín handed his grandfather the remaining oyster. "I think this is the one."

Zaragosa chuckled and drew a weathered hand down his beard. "And the others? You didn't think they were the ones?"

Manolín frowned. "This one was deeper. Hidden in a sandy part of the reef. It was the only one."

The old man remembered the sandy stretch between the reef and the island. It was where he had found many of the oysters that day. Maybe those were the ones with the pearls. Maybe the sand was the secret.

He shucked the oyster and heard the boy gasp.

"A pearl, *Papi!* A real live pearl. I knew it!"

Perched on the belly of the oyster was a small white orb the size of a papaya seed. It was perfectly round and as white as the beaches of San Evaristo.

"Muy bien," Zaragosa said, hiding his disappointment at the shape and color of the pearl. "An excellent find and a perfect way to end your first day as a pearl diver." He reached out his good arm and patted the boy on the back. "I am proud of you."

"A pearl diver," Manolín repeated, beaming with pride, and leaped back into the water.

❦ ❦ ❦

Roscoe and Tawny spent all morning on the wrong side of the island. It was the lee side of the island with the rocky coast where they'd come across the yellow bag, the bag that had whipped around the island with the storm current and the hurricane winds.

By early afternoon, Roscoe's head had stopped throbbing and Tawny had tired of fishing the coastline, one eye on the skipping lure, the other on the horizon in hope of spotting a fleet of oyster-harvesting *pangas.* The horizon remained empty.

"Maybe we should try the other side," Tawny said, reeling in the untouched lure.

"Can't hurt."

"I'd rather we were hunting snook."

"I know, baby." Roscoe was beginning to doubt his earlier confidence about the pearls and felt a rising guilt about leaving Magdalena Bay in such haste. "A day or two and then if we strike out, we'll head right back."

As they rounded the point, they spotted a single *panga* anchored near the shore. A swimmer was emerging from the water. A young boy. An old *pangero* was helping him aboard.

Roscoe scrambled for their tote bag and freed a pair of binoculars. "Holy shit," he exclaimed after focusing them. "The kid's handing oysters to the old man!"

"No way."

"Way." He handed her the binoculars.

"He's opening them," she said. Minutes later she set down the binoculars. "It has to be them."

Roscoe gunned the engine.

"Wait!"

"But—"

"What's your plan? To just cruise up and start diving beside them?"

Roscoe eased back on the throttle.

"Let's head back to camp and load up on supplies," she said. "Come back and camp on the island. See what happens tomorrow."

"I say we go grab some oysters."

"The bar owner said they're rare. We're not touching them."

"Easy for him to say. He's got our best pearl. He owns a bar. And a boat. And a freaking plane. We own an old four-wheeler and a skiff. Shit."

"Is that what this is all about?" Tawny shook her head. "Money?"

Roscoe slumped his shoulders.

"We're here to do what's right, Roscoe. That's it, and not a goddamn thing more. I mean it. Do you understand?"

"Okay."

"Look at me."

Roscoe raised his head.

"I love you." She moved to the stern and placed a hand on his thigh. "I love you so much. More than money or pearls or any other temporary shit. We're explorers. Fishermen. Lovers. This little Baja trip has turned into a crazy wild and very cool adventure, and there's no one I'd rather experience it with. You're my man. My soul mate. Let's do this thing right."

Roscoe leaned forward and kissed her. "I'm sorry. I love you, too." He spun the boat and gunned the engine for San Evaristo.

CHAPTER TWENTY-SEVEN

La Paz, Baja California Sur

Fish arrived back at his boat in a heavy sweat, hoping to find Skegs sunning himself on the back deck with a pile of rented scuba gear and a wisecrack or two. Instead, he found an empty back deck with the tarped submarine and desultory fishing gear. The worried expatriate stepped aboard, feeling angry and defeated.

He removed his fish-skin cap and ran a rough hand through his long hair, glancing out at the bay and the sailboats moored with their bows pointing into the incoming tide as if tethered for a race to the islands. He closed his eyes and felt the worry settle into his midsection. Then he gave a heavy sigh and walked into the saloon, his stride slow and tired.

For the first time in years he considered tasting Skegs's mescal—out of curiosity as much as tempted by the alcoholism that had nearly killed him. Back before his exile. The never-ending buzz that kept him numb through those years after his wife's death. Followed too quickly by his good friend's fatal luck while conducting a marriage in the mountains of northern Arizona. The bishop filling in for an ill priest only to be struck and killed by lightning. The denial of the bishop's life insurance based on the "Acts of God" exclusion. The ensuing class-action lawsuit filed by Fish on behalf of the bishop and hundreds of other claimants killed by freakish rock slides and wind shears and even softball-sized hailstones. The legal bait and switch that snagged every organized religion that endorsed the exclusion by proxy, agreeing that God did in fact include Mother Nature and all her accoutrements and dangers.

The unexpected settlement. The agreement by the religions to participate in the plaintiff's award. One day's donations from each order. Worldwide. A collection of money from hundreds of millions of anonymous believers that equaled billions of dollars. Fish's record-setting forty percent contingency fee. Sudden wealth beyond any tort attorney's comprehension. Wealth that inspired death threats from religious fanatics. Zealots who wanted the man who sued God dead.

So the lawyer ran for the border. Burned his courtroom clothes and grew matching ponytails during his self-imposed exile on the sand-dune island and the relative peace of Magdalena Bay.

But now, the attorney-turned-vagabond felt like bursting open the bibulous floodgates. Fish longed to dive deep into a bender. How bad could it be? he thought as he approached the galley and the teakwood cabinet where Skegs kept his personal stash. He opened the hand-carved doors and stared at a forest of beautiful amber bottles. He was reaching for one when his cell phone rang.

"Fish here," he said distractedly.

"Listen up, motherfucker." He heard the bark of a young man, trying to act tough. "We've got your friend. You want him back, you pay us ten grand. Cash. This afternoon."

Fish's mouth was bone-dry, and his heart was pounding. His hand slid to the braided goatee that had grown long these last few years, his fingers falling to the metal crimp dangling at the end. Skegs was more important to him than he'd realized.

"You're the young fighter," Fish said into the phone, remembering that voice. "The one they call Mikey, right?"

Mikey didn't answer.

Fish continued. "That's a lot of money, Mikey."

"I know it is," Mikey said, sounding less sure of himself.

Fish waited.

"Fine then," Mikey said. "I'll go back and tell Tank. But he'll go crazy and just fuck him up even more."

"Wait," Fish said. "If I pay you, Skegs is left alone. No more beatings."

"Okay."

"Where?"

"I . . . ," Mikey hedged, not wanting to meet the man they were stealing from, but not wanting to stoke Tank's unpredictable anger. "I'll send someone to pick it up. But you short us or follow, and Tank will kill your friend. I don't think I can stop him." His voice dropped. "I'm sorry about all of this."

"I'll have the money," Fish said. "And I won't follow. How soon can the courier be here?"

"Who?"

"Your bagman. The guy who picks up the ransom."

"Oh, right," Mikey said. "He'll come to you, on your boat. Marina de La Paz. Fuel dock. He'll have a bag for you to put it in."

"How soon?"

"One hour."

"Okay."

"I'll do everything I can to protect your friend. But they're getting crazier by the hour."

"The big guy with the bald head?" Fish asked. "How are the wounds?"

"He's pretty sick from those spines."

"Infection's set in. Is he taking any medicine?"

"Beer mostly. Some painkillers."

"Ten grand?"

"Ten grand," Mikey repeated.

"You should seriously think about distancing yourself from those two."

Mikey was quiet for a moment, then said, "I know."

"You're smarter than both of them put together. I saw it at the dock. Before they burned the bar. You're better than that. You know it and I know it."

"Please pay the money or they'll hurt him. I've tried to make them understand, but they won't listen."

"One hour," Fish said. "Ten grand. Make sure they know I said not to hurt him or I will send every cop and detective and drug cartel assassin after them. Quote me on that."

"Okay."

Fish pocketed his cell phone and shut the cabinet door. He walked to the back deck, yanked open the small refrigerator, and pulled out a soda. He popped the top and took a long, burning swallow as he looked out at the boats again, his eyes watering from the carbonation.

"Love you, brother," he said, toasting to Skegs's impending freedom.

Then he hurried inside the saloon to count out ten thousand dollars in ransom.

One hour later Fish watched from the helm of the *Fish Goddess* as a local kid waited for a boat owner to open the gate to the dock, then casually squeezed through before it clanged shut. The kid walked fast to the *Goddess,* saw the empty back deck, and hopped aboard. He was peeking under the canvas tarp where the personalized submarine sat hidden from view when Fish flung open the helm door and called out *"Oye!"*

The boy banged his head against the top of the metal chock on his way to his feet. *"Lo siento,"* he apologized, rubbing his hairline as he stepped toward the stern. He held an empty paper grocery bag before him. A message was written on the outside of the bag.

Fish descended the stairs to the back deck and accepted the bag. He smoothed out the bag and read the note. The handwriting was neat, but the message was anything but:

Happy Sunday asshole. Paybacks r a bitch. As you know we got ur buddy. U want him back place the dough in the bag. Do it now. The kid dont know shit so dont waste your time. If you follow the kid or fuck this up in any way, the Injun gets the blade. Signed Tank and Jimbo.

Fish smiled at the note and its author's attempt to distance himself from the two thugs who'd dictated it to him.

"*Momento,*" he told the boy, and ducked into the boat's saloon with the bag. Moments later he returned with the bloated paper bag under his arm.

"They have my amigo," he said, handing the boy the bag of money and a hundred-dollar bill. The boy's eyes widened. "I want him back. Pay attention to the men who hired you. In case we need sketches."

The boy nodded. "But there is only one gringo."

Fish nodded. "That you've seen. But there are two others."

The boy shrugged.

"A big guy with a missing tooth," Fish said. "He may be sick with fever. The other has a bad arm."

"Okay."

Fish looked away in case they were watched. "*Cuidado, niño.* These men are dangerous. I can protect you, but only if we play smart."

"Like chess?"

"Yes, like chess."

"Then we must stay two steps ahead."

Fish smiled but did not turn. "Yes, two steps ahead. Is the man who hired you driving an old beat-up RV?"

"No, señor. He's waiting in a cab around the corner."

Fish fought the urge to take his machete and force Baby-Face to lead him to the Winnebago. But then what? The fighters could be armed. And even if he did find the Winnebago, Skegs could be killed in the ensuing confrontation. The kidnappers were edgy and drunk—three boneheads-turned-arsonists-turned-kidnappers in a foreign country. An aggressive assault could lead to a bloodbath. It would be reckless.

Fish turned finally and looked toward the small parking lot in case Baby-Face was out of the cab watching, but he saw no one. He turned back toward the boat's saloon. "Pay close attention to which direction the cab goes."

"*Sí, señor,*" the boy said. "They are pawns in our game of chess."

"Dangerous pawns, *niño.* Do not forget that."

The boy pocketed the folded hundred-dollar bill. "*Gracias,*" he said, and tucked the bag of money under his arm. He raced down the dock and disappeared around the gate.

Fish paced the deck as he waited for his cell phone to ring with the anticipated sound of Skegs's voice and the news that he was free. After thirty minutes he gave up waiting and called Skegs's number.

"'Bout time, cocksucker!" came the booming, drunken voice that Fish remembered as the bald-headed bully's.

"This must be Tank."

"Fuck you."

"Where's Skegs?"

"Tied up at the moment."

"I want to talk to him."

"Here's what you're going to do instead. Another ten grand and he's all yours."

"I already paid the ransom."

"That was a test."

"Your credibility's suspect at this point."

The phone went dead.

Fish redialed.

Tank said, "You ready to pay, asshole?"

"I want to talk with Skegs."

"Who?"

"The Indian," Fish said coldly.

"Mikey said you ID'd him, too," Tank slurred, ignoring Fish's demand. "Don't fucking matter. He's coming back for the other ten. You pay or we cut off the Injun's ear."

"You think I just carry around twenty grand in cash? The first ten was a scramble," Fish lied. "It's Sunday. The banks aren't open."

"Not my problem."

"It is if you want cash."

Fish heard muffled noises and knew the kidnapper had covered the phone with his hand and was negotiating with his cohorts.

"Tomorrow then," Tank said. "You have until noon."

"Not unless I hear his voice."

Fish heard more shuffling sounds.

"Say something!" he heard Tank yell.

"You're dumb and ugly as dirt!" came the sound of Skegs's voice.

The phone went dead and Fish smiled. Skegs's feistiness would keep things interesting. The kidnappers were amateurs, and the lie about the money added time to the bargain. Time that worked against the drunken leader with the infected scalp. Fish had lied because he knew if he paid the second demand of ten thousand dollars, the kidnappers would demand a third and maybe a fourth. He quickly dialed a stateside number.

"Atticus?" the woman answered.

"Hey, Tooz," Fish said quietly. "I'm really sorry to bother you."

"Uh-oh. You sound serious."

"Got a bit of a problem."

"Where are you?"

"We're in La Paz."

"We?"

"Skegs is in trouble. Somebody nabbed him here."

Toozie took an audible breath. "Nabbed him? As in kidnapped him?"

"I paid ten thousand in ransom, but they refuse to let him go. They're demanding another ten grand."

"Random kidnappings are rare in Baja."

"It wasn't random."

She waited.

"I think it's related to the bar burning down the other night."

"Cantina del Cielo?!" Toozie exclaimed.

"A group of thugs came through with bad intentions. We ran them out of town. They came back in the middle of the night. The pearls might be related."

"Pearls?"

"A couple of tourists had them. Purple-hued and beautiful. One had a crooked edge. Almost tear-shaped. And big. Mesmerizing in the light. Magnificent, really."

"You're in the pearl business?"

"Not exactly," Fish said, breaking his thoughts from the fiery pearl. "The oyster-saving business actually. I think they're related to the famous strain that sent the Spaniards into fits centuries ago. It seems the fever continues. Someone stole them while I was working on the fire."

"I'm sorry to hear about the bar. Is everyone okay?"

"It was late. After closing. Chuy flew off, and I grabbed Pancho and Lefty before the palapa crashed down."

"Oh my God. The lizards. That would have been awful."

"And now they have Skegs."

"Was there a ransom note?"

"Kind of."

"Read it to me."

"I can't. It was on the paper bag. The one with the money in it. They took it back."

"They came directly to you for the ransom?"

"Sent a local kid."

Toozie sighed loudly. "These guys are amateurs. What did you say about the extra ten thousand?"

"Told them that I needed time to get the money from the bank. They gave me until noon tomorrow."

"I'll take the morning flight. Don't do anything until I get there."

"I can't ask you to do that."

"You didn't."

"Are you sure you can drop everything just like that?"

"I'm sure."

"Thank you."

"Do you know what kind of shape Skegs is in?"

"He sounded pissed off."

"You spoke with him?"

"Told the kidnappers I wouldn't pay another penny unless I knew he was okay. They made him shout into the phone and then hung up."

"Can you get hold of them again?"

"They're using Skegs's cell phone."

"Okay. I want you to call and make another demand. Tell them you want a photo of Skegs sent to your iPhone. A close-up of his face. Tell them that he better not be injured."

"I can guarantee he's injured," Fish said resignedly. "These guys are wannabe UFC fighters. We humiliated them. Locked them in a shark cage and nearly drowned them. Plus, there was blood on the floor at the shop where he was kidnapped."

"Shark cage?"

"Long story."

"You own a shark cage?"

"I'm not so good with downtime."

"I'm not sure I want to know."

"Research. To see if the sharks really are making a comeback."

"Research is one thing, but revenge can be costly, Atticus. You of all people should know that."

Fish let out a long breath as his fingertips found one of his recently healed bullet wounds. "It's not that easy when bullies come into town."

"I know, but this time it's Skegs who's paying the price."

Atticus did not respond.

"How much blood was at the shop?"

"Just a few drops. Like maybe they punched him in the face or something."

"Did you talk to the shop owner?"

"The place was abandoned. I had to break in."

"Are the police involved?"

"Not as far as I know."

The phone was silent for a few seconds, and Toozie said, "Atticus?"

"Still here."

"I know you meant well, and I know you'd do anything to protect your friend. But no heroics now, okay?"

"Okay."

"Go on a boat ride. Go chum for sharks. Go do anything but sit around and stew. I'll be there soon. In the meantime, no Rambo crap."

"Rambo?"

"MacGyver, Rockford, Dirty Harry. You know what I mean."

"What I know is that you're dating yourself."

Toozie ignored him. "The flight gets in late morning. Where are you staying?"

"Marina de La Paz. Tied up out by the fuel dock."

"You're on a boat?"

"The *Fish Goddess*. We were planning to use the sub to find the oyster bed. Try to save it before it's too late."

"Too late?"

"I'll pay the locals *not* to harvest the oysters. Any new bed will be fragile. A fleet of *pangeros* could wipe it out in weeks."

"A man of your worth and you're smitten with a few pearls."

"Smitten's an interesting choice."

Toozie gave a short laugh. "Once we get Skegs back, you can hunt all you want for pearls."

"You could stick around and help us."

Toozie didn't answer right away. After a moment she said, "You're a good man, Atticus. But there are things we need to work out."

"I know."

Toozie waited.

"Soon, I promise," Fish said quietly.

Toozie didn't respond.

"Toozie?" Fish said, staring across the bay and absentmindedly tugging at his braided goatee.

"I'm still here."

"If they hurt him, all promises are off."

"I know," she said.

CHAPTER TWENTY-EIGHT

Marina de La Paz, Baja California Sur

Fish checked the angle of the sun. Late afternoon. He walked inside the saloon and sent a text to Skegs's phone demanding a photograph proving that the mescal-maker was unharmed.

Fuck you was the immediate response.

No money until I see the photo

You get the money we send the photo

He better be okay

He slipped and hit his head when we got him. Little bit of a black eye

Prove it

Money first

You can't win this

Noon tomorrow 10 large

Photo

Tomorrow

Fish set the phone to the galley bar, anger welling up in his chest. The kidnappers wouldn't respond until the banks opened in the morning, and Toozie was still a day away. It was too much time to sit idle but plenty of time to head to Isla San Jose. He could do a little pearl reconnaissance to pass the time and see if word of the oyster bed had spread. The wind was light, and with a flat ocean he could be there at the island by sunset. Circle the island a few times and be back by sunrise.

Toozie had said no heroics, and he'd agreed. Reluctantly he kept his promise.

He climbed the helm ladder and engaged the twin engines. Then he freed the dock lines and slowly motored from the marina. With Toozie's help, he knew they'd rescue Skegs and permanently reroute the kidnappers north. The blood at the dive shop worried him, but it wasn't enough to indicate a serious wound. So unless the kidnappers were bluffing and his best friend was dead, Skegs would survive the ordeal. After all, the man could charm the hiss off a snake. Not that charm would be much good against these guys.

As the bay opened to a welcoming sea, Fish felt the stress of the last few days lessen. The bar would be rebuilt and the pearls protected. Skegs would return to his annoying ways—and hopefully Toozie would stay this time.

Fish floored the throttles and felt his spirits rise as the trawler lifted to plane.

CHAPTER TWENTY-NINE

Isla San Jose, Baja California Sur

Roscoe and Tawny made it back to Isla San Jose and by late afternoon had settled onto a peak overlooking the oyster reef with the single *panga* and the old man and the boy.

"I can't believe they're still here," Tawny said. "The kid must be exhausted."

"He must have gills."

They had hiked up from the opposite side of the island and carefully descended to their current vantage point, chosen for its large craggy boulders. There was just enough flat ground behind the boulders to unroll two sleeping bags. They had a gallon of water and a small cooler of beer. For food they had two cans of ravioli they planned to eat cold, as they'd agreed not to light a campfire. Better to remain hidden until they had more information.

"Beer?" Roscoe asked, opening the cooler for a Pacifico.

Tawny didn't answer. Instead, she raised a set of binoculars and swallowed a sharp gasp.

"Did they find a pearl?"

"The rich guy. Atticus. That's his yacht on the horizon."

Roscoe choked on a swig of beer.

Tawny shuffled back from the boulder and handed him the binoculars. "Take a look. I'm sure that's his boat."

Roscoe handed her the beer and took the binoculars. "Son of a bitch," he said, and lowered the glasses. "I knew he wasn't going to San Evaristo. Fucker's been in on it the whole time."

"We don't know that."

"He's coming straight for the old man and the kid."

"Maybe he's curious like us."

"Bullshit." Roscoe reached for his fanny pack and squeezed the fabric until he felt the two small pearls.

"You really think he was lying about wanting to save the oysters?"

"Don't you?"

Tawny shook her head and then drained half the beer. She belched away from the sea below and said, "It was too random, us showing up and him reaching into the tackle box and finding the yellow bag. No way he's in on it."

"That was days ago. He could have found out who lost the pearls and then joined up with them."

"An old man and a boy? They don't even have a radio on that *panga*. How do you think he contacted them?"

"How the hell should I know? He's here, isn't he?"

"I say we watch and see what he does. Think of it like a stakeout." She drained the beer. "Split another one?" She held up the empty.

"Might as well," Roscoe grumbled, and moved in a low crouch from the rock to the cooler.

❧ ❧ ❧

The afternoon sun flamed out behind the low mountains of southern Baja. Fish hardly noticed. He'd spotted a late-working *panga* off the northern end of Isla San Jose with its forbidding cliffs and rocky shoreline.

The oval-shaped island stretched for twenty miles at its longest and a half mile at its narrowest width. At less than a mile from the village of San Evaristo on Baja's eastern shore, the massive uninhabited rock created a channel frequented by boaters, mostly local *pangeros* and gringo sailors, but also the occasional fishing cruiser or yachtsman. It had a few small beaches and many shallow stretches of coastline. It was also prone to winds severe enough to sink a craft of any size.

Today, however, the winds were low and Fish had considered hugging the island's lee side. Now he was glad he hadn't. The ocean side of the island, with its heavier waves and deeper rocky bottom, was more likely to hold a secret reef. It was more likely to be unmolested by fishermen who'd prefer the shallower sandy bottom and fewer waves to lay their nets.

He grabbed the most powerful of his set of binoculars and focused in on the *panga*. It lay anchored in the falling light, its captain older with a cast over his right arm. The man was bent awkwardly over the bow, awaiting a swimmer returning from a dive. Fish adjusted the magnification and saw the swimmer's snorkel cutting through the water. Moments later Fish's heart pounded against his rib cage as he watched the swimmer hand an oyster to the captain.

Fish pushed the throttles to full power and minutes later reached the anchored *panga*. He slowed the engines to reduce the wake and stepped out from the helm. The gray-bearded captain stood suddenly and waved him off, his face stern and wrinkled and glistening with sweat. Fish saw the swimmer wriggle over the *panga*'s low gunwale, fast and agile.

A boy.

The captain shouted something in Spanish. Fish pulled the throttles to neutral, spun the wheel, and waited for the trawler to coast to a stop near the side of the *panga*.

Fish descended the helm ladder and walked to the bow. He introduced himself in Spanish, using the formal form of address, but the captain did not respond. Fish turned his attention to the boy, who shivered in the cool dusk.

"That oyster," he continued politely, "will it contain a purple pearl like the others?"

The captain's face darkened, but the boy's eyes grew wide with surprise.

"I don't want them," Fish said. "I am here only to protect them. I will pay you much more not to harvest them."

The boy looked at the captain, who seemed confused by Fish's offer. "We are fishermen," the old man stated without emotion. "The oysters are for market. There are no pearls."

"A plastic yellow bag with tinfoil holding pearls. It was you who lost it."

Fish saw the captain's mouth loosen and his tired eyes twitch. The man said nothing.

Fish continued. "Tell me how many pearls were inside the foil, and your grandson can return to school. And you, *Capitán*, can retire a rich man."

The old man scratched at his beard with his good hand. "I know nothing of this yellow bag or the tinfoil you speak of."

Fish shrugged and took a step toward the stern.

"Papi!" the boy cried out. "How could he know?"

Fish turned back and caught the captain's anguished look. "What is your name, young man?" Fish asked, addressing the boy in Spanish.

"Manolín."

Fish bowed respectfully. He turned to the captain. "And you, señor?"

"Zaragosa."

"Mucho gusto, Zaragosa y Manolín. Tourists came to my cantina in Puerto San Carlos. They had the yellow bag. They said they found it snagged on the rocks out here at the island."

"Where are these tourists now?" Zaragosa asked.

"I don't know."

Zaragosa's face fell.

Fish quickly added, "But they agreed to have one of the pearls tested. The big one. To see if they were authentic La Paz pearls, or if they were cultured somewhere else. Maybe in Guaymas." He paused and said, "But then it was stolen."

"Stolen?" Zaragosa asked with alarm.

"Someone must have overheard us. Someone desperate enough to burn down my cantina to get it."

The heavy skin around Zaragosa's eyes furrowed. "And yet you are here. Do you expect these criminals to come here?"

Fish shook his head. "I think they ran for the border. But I know what they look like. I will find them."

Zaragosa was silent for a moment. "It seems you came a long way to protect something you don't own."

"I have spent my life fighting injustice. I've been lucky. Time and money are not what they used to be. My life is now devoted to fighting greed."

"A luxury an old *pangero* like me can never enjoy, señor."

Fish asked for a moment and went below deck. When he reemerged, he held a thick roll of hundreds bound tightly by a rubber band. He tossed the money to the old man.

Zaragosa caught the offer in his good hand. Then he gave a hollow laugh and tossed it back. "Pull the anchor, Manolín."

The boy didn't move.

Fish let his eyes drift to where the boy had emerged earlier with the oyster and casually pitched the wad of money. It splashed into the darkening sea and slowly sank.

Manolín leaped over the gunwale and swam fast, disappearing and sinking beneath the surface.

Zaragosa glowered at Fish. "That was cruel."

"That boy should be in school, not here as night falls doing your bidding."

"That is not your concern."

"I don't blame you for not trusting me. To you I'm just another arrogant gringo with too much money. Too much free time. I get it. But I'm not your average *norteamericano*. I actually give a shit."

Zaragosa chewed at his mustache. "So you say."

"I lost your pearl. That money your grandson is diving for is partial payment for my stupidity. Take it. Come to Puerto San Carlos. Visit my *restaurante* when it reopens. Meet the local people I employ. Ask them if they trust me. Do the research. But in the meantime please leave the oysters where they are. I will pay you *not* to harvest them. If you decide I am not who I say I am, then take the oysters. Destroy the only bed left in all of southern Baja. It will then be on your conscience, not mine."

"You want to pay me not to harvest these oysters?"

"To protect this bed."

"From who?"

"Anyone snooping around."

A commotion on the surface caught their attention, and they turned to see Manolín emerge from the depths with a wide grin.

Zaragosa turned back to Fish. "You do not own this island. We are free to take what we want from this water."

"Yes, of course. But pearl oysters were thought extinct. I'd like to see them survive. See the curse of Mechudo ended once and for all." At the mention of the Legend of Mechudo, the old man's brow hitched high. Fish saw it and asked, "How much for you not to harvest them?"

Zaragosa considered the idea. "If the fishing is good, I can make one hundred dollars a week."

"Then I will pay you twice that. For not harvesting the oysters and making sure no one else does."

"How many others know?"

"The tourists who found the yellow bag, my partner and I, and the thief and anyone he might've told. If any of them come looking, warn them away. Tell them the area is a protected sanctuary."

"And if they ignore us, or fight us? We are not soldiers."

Fish nodded. "Then trick them away. You are a smart man; I can tell."

"I will need help. And anyway, the other *pangeros* will suspect something if I have money without fishing. Especially once my arm is healed."

"Include those you trust. I will pay as many men as you need. But you must keep an eye on this place. Tell the other *pangeros* that you've been hired by the gringo who owns Cantina del Cielo in Puerto San Carlos. That I've hired you to protect something precious. They will know of Mechudo. They will cooperate. I will anchor off your village later this week to prove it to them."

"And what is under the tarp?" Zaragosa pointed at the trawler's back deck.

"A submarine."

Zaragosa laughed. Manolín pulled himself aboard the *panga* and held out the wet wad of money. Zaragosa patted him on the head. "Say hello to my new boss, Manolín."

Manolín shook the water from his head and gave a shivery smile. "To find the pearls?"

"To protect them."

Manolín's eyes widened.

Fish opened a compartment near the bow rail and tossed the boy a towel. "I might need a young deckhand, too. On weekends. A deckhand who's good at keeping a secret."

"I can keep secrets," Manolín said excitedly.

CHAPTER THIRTY

La Paz, Baja California Sur

Bart Kraken slipped aboard the thirty-two-foot *Reel Cool* like a night owl, his opaque eye glowing amber in the moonlight, his other black as doom. The back deck of the old boat was dark and cluttered with the detritus of his worthless partner's dying charter business. Old tackle boxes, trays of rusty lures, a threadbare life jacket. Half a dozen fishing rods stood bungeed into the corner near the helm ladder, their reels filled with yellowed monofilament, their eyelets frayed and salt-ridden. A wood-handled filet knife drooped in the darkness, its point buried into the cracked and peeling gunwale. Near the stern, a fighting chair held an empty bottle of Don Julio tequila, a plastic Dixie cup spilled across the worn seat cushion. A crumpled Taco Loco bag soaked up most of the lost tequila. Amidships, the saloon door stood ajar.

Kraken knew the old fisherman was passed out inside, fully dressed in his stained sweatshirt and sweat-lined fishing cap. Kraken had spotted the eight-cylinder two-toned brown 1973 Buick Riviera parked out front. He knew that the man was too drunk to drive, probably too drunk to remember where he'd parked the relic of a car. Kraken dreaded getting behind the wheel. The vehicle was an embarrassment for a self-respecting businessman like himself. A diesel truck with dually tires and a Blaupunkt sound system was the ticket—a ride that Kraken planned to purchase with his soon-to-be-stolen ransom money. He would bury the three overconfident muscle-heads one at a time. Maybe take them out on the old man's boat and chum them for the hammerheads. After he dissolved his partnership with the old man and helped himself to the keys of that abomination of a Buick.

Kraken glanced around the deserted dock and then ducked into the saloon. The codger was on his back, snoring loudly from the fore-cabin bunk, his filthy bare feet hanging off the end. Kraken reached over toward the starboard window and freed a cushion from the couch. The air inside the saloon smelled of sweat and booze and half-eaten tacos.

Kraken took a deep breath and had just stepped forward when the sound of a bell echoed across the room. Kraken froze. Then the nautical clock repeated itself. Kraken waited, his muscles taut, his nerves on alert for the slightest movement. Nothing but rhythmic snores. Nine times the clock tolled, and each time Kraken felt his anger rise. It was an anger quelled only by the knowledge that they would be the last nine chimes of the old man's shitty existence.

Kraken lunged.

The old man jerked. He flailed his arms uselessly against Kraken's smothering weight. His fists landed weakly, his screams muffled by the moldy cushion. Kraken wrapped his legs and squeezed. He felt the old man's feet flutter as if swimming underwater. He felt the convulsions, the final thrust, and then the stillness.

Kraken counted silently to thirty, keeping pressure on the cushion. Then another thirty seconds before rolling free. Slowly he stood and backed up from the bunk, listening for sounds on the dock. Nothing. He remained still in case the old man came to life. There was only the gentle lapping of the outgoing tide against the hull. Kraken felt his muscles relax, his heart slow. A feeling of power washed over him so suddenly that he almost grunted with satisfaction. Instead, he closed his eyes and thought of the plan he'd just put into motion. He thought of the easy money in front of him and of the lesson he'd soon teach those idiots who'd dared burst into his shop and threaten him.

He opened his eyes and surveyed the dark room. Shadowy light filtered in from the tiny lights at the top of the neighboring boat masts. He couldn't recall his senses ever being this acute. The night breeze brought the scent of the marina. He could taste the coppery smell of seawater rushing out beneath him, could feel the creosote of the dock planking on his skin, the acrid waft of bird droppings. Every night sound was amplified: cleat lines creaking like steel cables; barnacles crunching against cement pilings, pinched by the falling tide and the lowering dock; canvas spinnakers snapping in the breeze.

Kraken straightened. His mind raced. The old man had friends, drunks who might stop by for a morning chat. Complain about petty bullshit over a breakfast cocktail. Bitch about the tourists, the locals, the corrupt politicians on both sides of the border. What a shock it would be for them to find their drinking pal a bit stiffer than usual. He thought of the faux sadness and the ensuing gossip. And then the authorities called in to investigate.

A dead gringo at Marina de La Paz would attract attention. Even if it was ruled a heart attack, or a stroke, or whatever the coroner felt like listing as the cause of the geezer's death. Someone would surely visit the dead man's apartment, collect his valuables, maybe impound the old Buick and his piece-of-crap boat. Kraken couldn't let any of that happen. Not until he'd appropriated his earnings from the three thugs.

Kraken strolled casually to the back deck and stepped to the dock where he quickly untied the cleat lines. He hopped back aboard and climbed the helm ladder, smiling when he saw the key in the ignition. The old man never removed it. Never saw the need. Marina de La Paz was safe. Nobody stole boats. At least not crappy gringo boats whose owners were still alive.

Kraken turned the key, and the diesel engine coughed to life. He chugged from the marina under the wan glow of the mast lights. A night heron squawked its annoyance at the nighttime departure.

Once outside the marina, he dialed his cell phone.

"Change of plan," he told the man who answered on the first ring.

"Fuck you," Tank said.

"Bad night?"

"What change of plan?"

"Meet me at the old cemetery around midnight. It's around the corner from the dive shop. Ask around. You'll find it."

"I don't like cemeteries."

"That's the point. Nobody does. That's where we make the switch. You leave the Winnebago and we take the Buick back to my partner's apartment. Count the ransom money and part ways."

"I can live with that," Tank said. "But why midnight? Let's do it now."

"Got an errand to run."

"Sounds like you're on a boat. Where the fuck are you?"

Kraken ignored the question. "Brown two-toned Buick. You can't miss it. Midnight."

He disconnected the call and gunned the engine. Pichilingue Bay was a twenty-minute boat ride from Marina de La Paz. The deepwater channel to the ferry port was the ideal spot for dumping a body. There would be nobody around late on a Sunday night. An outgoing tide would wash the dead man's body out to sea.

Afterward, he'd tie off at the *panga* dock and take a taxi back to Marina de La Paz. Get the Buick and head to the cemetery. Pretend to be a team player while secretly setting the trap to exact revenge on anyone stupid enough to barge into his dive shop and kidnap one of his customers.

To kill anyone stupid enough to fuck with Bart Kraken.

CHAPTER THIRTY-ONE

La Paz, Baja California Sur

Tank tossed the cell phone to the dashboard of the Winnebago and wiped the sweat pouring from his head. He reached down and adjusted the bag of ten thousand dollars taped to his calf for safekeeping.

"Who was on the phone?" Mikey asked.

"Dive shop dude. Said we're meeting at midnight to switch cars and head to the hideout."

When Mikey didn't respond, Tank turned toward the back where Jimbo lay snoring, sprawled across the threadbare couch. Skegs was still taped to the lawn chair, which in turn had been taped to one of the legs of the couch. The skin around his eye had bruised, and dried blood caked his temple. Mikey sat next to Skegs, feeding him half a burrito and soda through a straw.

"Don't feed him too much," Tank said. "We don't need any more puke next time around."

Mikey nodded, then shot an uneasy glance at Jimbo, who hadn't stirred since passing out two hours earlier. He looked back at Tank. "The rich guy said no injuries. He won't pay any more without a photo. Come on, Tank. Can't we just get out of here? I think this guy's had enough already."

"Who the fuck asked you?"

Mikey shrugged. "We came here to train. Not get caught up in a bunch of crazy criminal enterprises."

"These assholes started it. We're finishing it."

"The guy already paid us ten grand. Seems like we're doing more than just finishing it."

At the mention of the money, Tank checked his calf for the umpteenth time. Satisfied it was still there, he sucked air through the gap of his missing tooth and asked, "Mikey, what does a fighter do when he's punched?"

"He punches back."

"How many times?"

"Until his opponent falls. But—"

"But shit. My head hurts from that goddamn cactus, and my lungs are fucked up from nearly drowning inside that fucking shark cage. The opponents haven't fallen yet. But they will."

Mikey sighed.

The phone rang again. "Yo," Tank said, sinking back into the driver's seat. "Uh-huh. Roger that." He hung up and without turning said, "That was the Canadian dude. I almost forgot about him. Says he's pulling in soon. Wants the scuba gear."

Mikey's shoulders slumped. "We've got enough money, Tank. Let's forget about it. Let this guy go and get back on the road." He ran a hand along his lizard scratches. "Plus, I don't trust that dive shop owner. Those weird eyes and that god-awful greasy hair. Gives me the creeps."

Tank reached into the cooler, pulled a can of beer from it, and pressed it to his burning scalp, rolling it back and forth across the open sores. "Get a cab, Mikey, and take the scuba stuff to Marina de La Paz. It's an easy score. Make sure he pays you the five hundred bucks he promised. All of it. Up front. Cash."

"And then what?"

"And then get your ass back here. By noon tomorrow we'll have another ten large."

Skegs spoke up. "You're fucking with the wrong cat."

"Is that so," Tank muttered.

"You keep pounding on me and Fish'll hunt you down and make your meaningless life even more miserable than it is now.

He's probably already hired half the cops in La Paz to find this piece of shit we're hiding in."

Tank coughed out a painful laugh. "I'm starting to like you, Geronimo."

"Name's Skegs. And he will find you."

Tank opened the beer, chugged half, then turned in his seat. "Don't fucking threaten me. Your rich pal knows we burned his bar to the ground. He won't hire any fucking cops. Want to know why?"

Skegs didn't answer.

"Because he attacked us first. He started this shit. You know it. We know it." Tank finished the beer.

"He said no more ransom unless he sees a photo of me unharmed. What do you think he's going to do when he sees a photo of my face?"

"I'm planning to send him a profile."

"You think you can fool him just like that? Man, you have a lot to learn."

Tank fished out another beer. "It'll work."

Mikey started to argue, but Skegs interrupted. "Say you get the money, tough guy. Then what? Only one road out of Baja."

"They got airports. Maybe we'll fly first class."

"Not without a passport."

"Who says we ain't got passports?"

"Because they don't give passports to apes."

Tank's face tightened.

"Don't do it," Mikey said. "He's trying to bait you."

Without taking his eyes off Skegs, Tank said, "Get the cab, Mikey. Take the gear to the marina. You've got one hour."

Mikey turned to Skegs, who held Tank's glare without blinking. "Can't you see Tank isn't feeling well?" he murmured to him. "Don't press him."

Skegs didn't respond.

"The clock's running, Mikey," Tank growled, rivers of sweat falling down his forehead.

Mikey blew out a long breath and went to the side door of the Winnebago and flung it open. He glanced back at the two men still locked in a death stare, then slammed the door and went looking for a cab.

⚜ ⚜ ⚜

Mikey made it to Marina de La Paz in less than thirty minutes, and found the pale-skinned Canadian sitting at the Dockside Restaurante and drinking a glass of white wine. Ten o'clock on a Sunday night and the room was empty, but for the bartender and his one customer.

"Something to drink, eh?" Angus asked, motioning the bartender over.

"No, thanks."

Angus waved the man away. "Where are your buddies?"

"The gear's outside," Mikey said, without answering the question. "Want me to help load it onto your boat?"

Angus sipped his wine. "Why the long face? Can't be the lizard scratches. They look better than expected."

"The guy whose bar we burned down." Mikey glanced around nervously, fingering the scabs within his patchy sideburns. "He's here."

Angus sat up straight. "Here?"

"Actually, out there." Mikey pointed through the bank of windows overlooking the docks. "On his boat. Tied up near the fuel dock."

Angus relaxed. "Nothing's tied up there now. I would have seen it coming in. How sure are you?"

"Positive."

"How positive?"

Mikey narrowed his eyes. "Hundred percent. Which is why I'd like to load the gear and get the hell out of here."

"But why would the bar owner be here?"

"The Indian said he was looking for us."

"You talked to Skegs?"

"You know him?" Mikey asked with surprise.

"You could say that."

Angus moved so fast, Mikey never saw the knife until its sharpened tip poked through his T-shirt and pricked his lower rib cage.

"You've got five seconds to spill it," Angus hissed.

Eyes wide as saucers, Mikey croaked, "Nothing to spill. I swear to God."

Angus eased back on the knife. "Start talking. If I like what you say, I put the blade away. If not, the bartender's going to need a bigger mop."

Mikey quickly explained running into the Indian at the dive shop and how Tank and Jimbo went crazy with revenge. How they turned even meaner when he tried to reason with them. How Tank was sick with infection and obsessing about the ransom money while ignoring the obvious risk.

"You're saying you don't trust your friends anymore?" Angus asked, sheathing the knife.

"They've changed," Mikey said. "For the worse."

"The rich guy paid the ransom? Just like that?"

"Only because Tank promised to release the Indian. It was a stupid double cross, though, because now the rich guy wants photos before he hands over any more money. Proof that his friend is all right."

"Is he?"

"They roughed him up some. Black eye. Maybe a few broken ribs." He shook his head miserably. "Enough that the rich guy's not going to like what he sees. The photo's going to cause us big problems."

Angus finished his wine in one long swallow and placed a hundred-peso note on the bar. He reached into the breast pocket of his Windbreaker and handed Mikey a roll of twenties.

"Good luck, kid," he said, and started for the scuba gear piled by the nearest dock gate.

Mikey hurried after him. "You searching for sunken treasure? Pirates used to lie in wait in this bay. Legends say galleons were scuttled with millions in gold and silver."

Angus stopped. "Say again?"

"Treasure," Mikey repeated. "Why else would you want all that scuba gear?"

"I like to spearfish."

"Nobody needs ten tanks and an air compressor to spearfish."

"Go back to your buddies and try to stay alive."

"I'm not going back." Mikey handed Angus the roll of twenties. "I'd rather earn your money by helping you find whatever it is you're looking for."

Angus stared at the money.

"The rich guy was out there," Mikey reminded him. "Wherever he went, I guarantee he'll be back. The quicker we get away the better."

"I like working alone," Angus said, but he did not turn away.

"I'm not as big as the other guys, but I can fight," Mikey said. "In case you need someone to guard your boat while you're down there . . . spearfishing or whatever."

Angus paused before speaking, his mind contemplating the risks in refusing the young man's offer, a young man desperate enough to cause trouble with rumors about sunken treasure. A desperate man aligned with two goons guaranteed to be caught by the rich bar owner. A bar owner Angus needed at all costs to avoid. The kid would mention the scuba gear and the sailboat and the Canadian captain. Skegs may have been drunk that night in the bar, but he'd surely remember the man with the accent asking questions about the bar owner. All of it circumstantial evidence placing him there the night the bar burned down when the pearl disappeared.

"You ever been on a sailboat before?" Angus asked, the nefarious plan forming as he spoke.

"No, but I'm a good swimmer."

Angus snatched the roll of twenties from Mikey's hand. "Good enough," he said. "Load the boat. We've got some sailing to do."

CHAPTER THIRTY-TWO

Sea of Cortez, Baja California Sur

After leaving Zaragosa and Manolín to formulate a plan for watching over the oyster bed, Fish tossed out a fishing line and trolled the falling light of the evening *crepúsculo* toward La Paz. As he rounded the south end of the island, the old Penn reel groaned with the heaviness of a bull dorado. As the thirty-pound fish leaped and tail-walked across the water, the sky fought hard to keep the remnants of kaleidoscope light from escaping.

Within minutes darkness swallowed the last of the sunset, and Fish landed the dorado. He didn't reach for the gaff or the fancy fish bat Skegs had bought him a year earlier. Instead, he uncapped a bottle of Skegs's Macho Mescal and poured it into the fish's gullet. The old Hawaiian trick worked almost immediately. Fish sprinkled the high octane booze over each gill plate and down its toothy maw. The result was as humane as it was effective. An angry bull dorado suddenly comatose. No brutal head blows aimed at a thick skull and a minuscule brain. No temporarily stunned fish quickly boated and come to life to wreak havoc across the deck. Fish had heard stories about big game fish thought dead, only to awaken and career wildly into unsuspecting anglers, breaking legs and arms or worse. Old-school Hawaiians, in their outrigger canoes landing enormous tuna and mahimahi, had discovered the perfect method for safeguarding their gear and their lives: rotgut vodka sprayed from a cheap plastic bottle. If death was imminent, Fish supposed an instantaneous overdose on booze wasn't a bad way out. Blissful asphyxiation beat a cracked skull as far as he was concerned. He was certain the game fish agreed.

As he recapped the mescal, the strong smell of the distilled cactus brought his thoughts back to Skegs. The man would be proud of this latest use of his product. Fish boated the limp dorado and felt the recently familiar guilt rise quickly. Skegs should have been here, whooping and hollering about the hookup. Making jokes about the state of the expatriate's fishing gear, the presentation of the lure, the dumb luck of the gringo. Instead, the happy-go-lucky mescal bootlegger was imprisoned somewhere in La Paz with a trio of madmen. Fish swallowed hard at the thought of the failed fighters using Skegs as a punching bag. The guilt turned to anger, and Fish made a vow to do more than save his friend. He made a personal promise to punish the kidnappers.

He quickly filleted the catch and, after a lonely dinner of fish tacos, was motoring full speed for Marina de La Paz. By midnight he was passing the island of Espíritu Santo with its deep finger bays and spectacular beaches. An hour later he slowed to wakeless speed inside the big bay and caught sight of the crooked-masted sailboat passing by on its way out to sea. Fish waved at the two shadowed men as they passed between the red and green channel buoys. Both men waved back. Dismissing a fleeting sense of déjà vu, Fish turned his attention to Marina de La Paz in the distance. Minutes later he tied up to the fuel dock and fell into a deep sleep until almost noon, waking only to a knock on the saloon door.

"You're not back on the sauce, are you?" Toozie asked when Fish opened the door, his long hair disheveled, his green eyes puffy with sleep.

Without replying, Fish reached out and pulled her into a hard hug. "I can't believe how much I missed you."

"I'm glad," she said.

"About last time—"

Toozie put a finger to his mouth and said, "Save it for later. We've got work to do. Any word from our kidnappers?"

Fish corkscrewed his mouth with a curt nod, and then reached into the zipper pocket of his sailcloth pants. "I haven't slept much," he said, checking the phone. "They were supposed to send a photo of Skegs. Nothing yet. But . . ." He paused. "I found the pearl divers."

Toozie waited.

"An old man and his grandson. They agreed to get some local *pangeros* and protect the bed." Fish couldn't help but smile. "They work for me now."

"You found them?" Toozie said with surprise. "How?"

"I'm not so good with downtime."

"I'm impressed."

"Our kidnappers will want the rest of the money soon."

"I suspect so."

"How do we play it?"

"Doesn't really matter."

Fish raised his brow and tugged at his braided goatee.

"Once they get the money, it's game over for them. We can take our time, depending on your state of mind."

"My state of mind is pissed off."

Toozie reached into her patchwork purse and handed Fish a half-dozen extra-wide rubber bands.

"What's this?"

"Tracker bands. Tiny chips inside each one that'll send us a signal. Unless they unwrap every bundle and toss the bands, we'll have them."

Fish smiled. "Did I mention how much I missed you?"

CHAPTER THIRTY-THREE

La Paz, Baja California Sur

"I knew it," Jimbo growled from a rickety chair at the center of the sparse studio apartment that served as their new hideaway. He downed his can of Modelo Light and crumpled it. "Stupid shit ran off with our five hundred bucks."

Tank shrugged. They'd met Bart Kraken at midnight at the cemetery and transferred their hostage and whatever belongings they remembered to the Buick. Kraken drove, and ten minutes later he pulled up to a decrepit apartment building and parked on the street. The one-room studio apartment was on the ground floor and stunk like unwashed clothes and ferment. A single bed with no sheets was pushed into the corner near the door to the bathroom. The kitchen was a cracked sink set to the wall just beneath the small window, and a mini refrigerator. Someone had nailed a sloping shelf to the yellowing drywall. The floor was undulating linoleum. A half-dozen ancient-looking scuba tanks stood upright in a corner. Broken fishing gear lay scattered everywhere.

Tank leaned uncomfortably against the lumpy pillows of the bed clicking through the channels of the black-and-white television propped on an end table. His scalp oozed pus. Sweat poured down his head. Every few minutes he reached down and touched the sweat-drenched paper bag filled with ten thousand dollars and taped against his calf.

"One less idiot to split our ransom money with," he said, patting the bag of money.

Kraken stood in the far corner near the scuba tanks, watching quietly. Skegs sat hunched and duct-taped to his lawn chair at the foot of the bed. The leg of the chair was now taped to the leg of the bed.

"Plus," Tank said, sucking air through his gap tooth, "we know where Mikey lives. Once we get back with our money, we're gonna open up a big fucking can of UFC whipass on little ol' Mikey."

"*Whoop*-ass," Skegs corrected, pulling covertly at his binds.

Tank dropped his hand from the remote control and balled his hand into a fist. "What the fuck did you just say?"

Kraken laughed coldly. "He said, it's *whoop*-ass, not *whip*-ass. Indian's smarter than he looks."

"You better shut the fuck up, freaky-eyed motherfucker."

Kraken gave a clipped grin and said, "I set you up in a sweet hideaway with a car, and you disrespect me like that?"

"Nobody corrects me, asshole." Tank swiped at a line of bloody pus working its way down one of his sideburns. "And this place ain't sweet, far as I'm concerned. It's a goddamn dump."

"A dump nobody knows about. You should be thanking me."

"You'll get your thousand bucks. Unless you keep siding with the Indian."

"I'm not siding with anyone."

Tank scowled. "Jimbo, get me a fresh beer. My head's fucking killing me."

"What you need is medicine," Kraken said, then went to the shelf beside the sink and rummaged among the cluster of plastic bottles. There were dozens of bottles with Spanish labels. Kraken remembered the old man complaining of his arthritis, saying that oxycodone was best. He had said half a pill was all it took to get him going in the morning. Another half at lunch. Add booze and the ride was better than sex. Maybe so, Kraken allowed. There wasn't a single bottle on the shelf with the words Viagra or Levitra.

"The old man has a pharmacy here," he added.

Jimbo stumbled to his feet and retrieved Tank a beer. He glared at Skegs. "Tell you what, this goddamn Indian needs a lesson in respect, Tank. Son of a bitch's gonna keep his trap shut when I get finished with him." He drained his beer and heaved the crumpled can at Skegs's head.

Skegs ducked, and the can bounced off Tank's chest.

Tank looked at his sweat-stained T-shirt and the beer foam dripping down his chest. He slowly directed his bloodshot eyes at Jimbo. "You must have a fucking death wish."

"Sorry," Jimbo said, handing Tank the fresh beer and raising his hands in surrender. He nodded his head toward Skegs. "Want me to bust his nose?"

"How fucking stupid are you two?" Kraken asked, uncapping a bottle of Demerol. "You bust his nose and you can forget about the photo you were talking about earlier."

Tank tossed his cell phone to Kraken, who spilled some of the pills as he snatched the phone from midair. "You take it," Tank said. "My head's starting to throb bad. Give me one of them pills."

Kraken set the phone on the sink and shook out a pill. "Chew it and chase it with a beer," Kraken said. "It'll kick in right away."

"Give me one of those fuckers," Jimbo said. "My arm's killing me," he lied, pointing to the thorn marks where the hunk of cactus had landed days earlier during the fiasco with the crazy rich dude. But the thorns hadn't infected him like they'd infected Tank. "It's all bruised up inside," he added.

"Bullshit," Tank said through gritted teeth. He swallowed the bitter pieces of the pill and slid upright on the bed so he could wash it down with beer. "You need to stay clearheaded when you go get our money."

Jimbo opened the cooler and grabbed himself a new can of beer. "Half a pill then?"

Tank rolled off the bed and slammed a fist into Jimbo's kidney.

Jimbo dropped to a knee, keeping the beer upright in his hand. "What the fuck was that for?" he wheezed.

"Payback for spilling beer on my shirt." Tank chugged his beer, sank back onto the bed, and belched. He turned to Kraken.

"Take a profile of his good side, Mr. Dive Dude. You show the black eye and I give you one."

Kraken glared, but then slowly raised the phone and aimed it at Skegs.

"Fuck a whole bunch of all of you," Skegs said, swiveling his head back and forth.

Tank lunged for him, crashing clumsily into Kraken on his way. "Easy there, Turbo," Kraken said, tossing him back onto the bed with surprising ease. He looked stunted next to Tank, but there was no denying the power in his hunched, misshapen shoulders, or the homicidal gleam in his freaky eyes as he turned to face Jimbo, who'd taken a step toward him. "Bring it," he said very softly to the much bigger man, his unbalanced eyes flickering darkly. "Please, fucking bring it."

Jimbo hesitated, then took a step back.

Kraken turned to Tank. "That medicine's kicking in. You take it easy, big man." He aimed the cell phone at Skegs. "Turn your head sideways, or I'll break each of your toes slowly. Starting with the big ones."

Skegs saw the gleeful anticipation in Kraken's scarred face and turned his head obediently. Kraken snapped the picture, then viewed the results with satisfaction. "He's never looked lovelier."

Tank sat up on the bed, then caught the same dangerous look from the man with the phone and fell onto his back again, his head spinning. "Send the photo, asshole," he managed so say. "Then go out and get me something to eat."

"You said his name was Fish, right?" Kraken scrolled through the list of names. "It's not in here."

Jimbo took a cautious step backward to his chair and said, "First name's Asskiss or some shit like that."

"Atticus," Kraken said, and punched the screen with a forefinger. "Sent." He pocketed the phone.

"Tell him we want the next ten grand now," Jimbo snarled.

Tank sluggishly fought himself to a sitting position against the pillows and in a faraway voice said, "You don't give orders, Jimbo."

"Sorry, boss."

Tank tried to focus on Kraken, who walked to the sink and poured a glass of water. "Tell him I want the ten grand now," he said, his eyes drooping as he spoke the last words.

"Already did," Kraken said, turning toward the window, his lips aslant with a vicious grin.

CHAPTER THIRTY-FOUR

Sea of Cortez, Baja California Sur

By the time Angus Black arrived at Isla San Jose, the sun was breaching a cloudless sky, and his new first mate was sound asleep in the fore bunk. No wind had greeted the sailors, and the sea remained a skintight suit of blue linen marred by an occasional dolphin cruising by or, as he neared the rocky shore of the island, a pelican jackknifing for baitfish. The dearth of wind had forced Angus to use the small outboard most of the night, emptying the first of his two gas tanks.

He adjusted his wide-brimmed hat and added a layer of sunscreen to his face and hands, the only skin exposed to the sun. He wore a pair of used Docksides he'd nicked from the dock in La Paz, salty jeans, and a sweaty long-sleeved shirt. And a fancy pair of polarized sunglasses taken from the deck of a yacht weeks earlier.

As he approached the south end of the island, Angus marveled at its size. Isla San Jose was no small rock. It was as long and wide and tall as any mountain in southern Canada. It was also obviously devoid of human life, at least on the side Angus could see. He knew nothing about oysters, but he'd assumed if pearls were around, he'd see activity of some sort—maybe a cluster of boats working the shallows. Instead, he saw only the empty canvas of water and an uninviting rocky shoreline.

He reached out to free the stolen binoculars hanging on a hook affixed to the main mast and removed his sunglasses. There were two lengthy sides of the island, one steep with cliffs, the other rising gently. Both were equally deserted. At least the general shoreline was, but to be sure he'd have to circle the entire island. He'd have to check all the coves, putting in hours of endless sailing. Angus cursed his bad luck. He'd already spent days getting here—hours of running the outboard. He'd even taken on a stranger who knew too much. And for what?

Angus realized now as he scanned the expanse of empty water just how impossible a task it would be to find pearls without any obvious signs of others doing the same. Treasure hunters anchored over a reef or stacked along a shoreline. Swimmers or divers splashing about the sea. Something, anything. But finding an oyster bed here in this wasteland of rock and water would be like finding a diamond in the sand.

Impossible.

Angus lamented his foolishness at thinking he could just sail to an unknown island and pick off a few pearl oysters. He once again scanned the inside channel and saw nothing. He scanned the open ocean side of the island. Nothing. As he went to lower the binoculars, he caught a glint near the north end of the island. It was not far from the base of a rock slide with a small beach, well over a mile away. He refocused the twin barrels of the glasses, but the glint had vanished. He waited. Nothing. Maybe it was the flash of a fish or a splash of seawater, or maybe it was a swath of mica on the rocks caught at just the right angle. He started to lower the glasses again, when a movement caught his eye. This time he saw it: a small canoelike boat tucked into the shadows of the island, an empty *panga* hiding in the shallows. Angus felt his heart spike.

"Hey, deckie!" he called out. "Get your ass up here!" He stomped on the deck to convey the urgency. "We got company, eh!"

Mikey sat up and banged his head against the bulkhead. "Huh?" he called out sleepily.

"We got a local hiding out up ahead."

Mikey appeared from below. "Hiding from who?" He rubbed the sleep from his eyes. "Man, I forgot what it was like to sleep. I could get used to this ocean stuff."

"I didn't hire you to sleep."

"Wasn't nothing going on."

"There is now."

"But why would locals be hiding way out here?"

Remembering Mikey's earlier comment about sunken treasure, he said, "Probably knows where the treasure is, and he doesn't want anyone else finding out about it."

"Except you already know about it, right?"

"Right."

Angus handed Mikey the binoculars, then gave the small outboard full throttle. The boat responded with a slightly faster chug, and an hour later they sidled up to a sea cave large enough to hold a small boat. The *panga* lay at anchor just inside.

"*Hola*," Angus called out.

An old Mexican fisherman with a broken arm rose from the floorboards where he'd been napping. The man yawned and ran a weathered hand down his gray beard.

"How's the diving around here?" Angus asked.

The man gave a blank stare. "*No hablo inglés.*"

Angus turned to Mikey. "You speak Spanish?"

Mikey shrugged. "A little bit."

Angus gave a disappointed scowl and went to the stern. He unclipped a scuba tank bungeed to the railing and raised it above his head. "Scuba diving," he said, slowly enunciating the words.

The old man shrugged. "*No bueno.*" He motioned in a circular fashion with his forefinger. "*Otro lado.*"

"What the fuck does that mean?" Angus said, and mimicked the old man's hand signal. "The whole island is good for diving?"

"I think he said the other side is better," Mikey said.

"The other side is better?" Angus called out to the old man, with another mimic of the hand gesture.

The old man nodded. "*Aquí es no bueno.*" He slashed a weathered palm in front of his neck. "*Nada.*"

"Okay," Angus said, and turned to Mikey. "Go set the anchor."

"What?"

"The anchor. It's at the front of the boat. Drop it overboard and tie the line off on the cleat. Tie it good and tight."

"But he said it's no good here."

"Which is why we're staying put."

Mikey cocked his head. "You think the old guy's putting us on?"

"I do indeed."

Mikey didn't look convinced.

"In my line of work, reading people's a lifesaving talent."

"I don't follow."

"Think, kid. It's early afternoon. This guy's old as dirt. His arm's in a cast. Why's he out here sleeping in a sea cave?"

"To rest in the shade. It's hot in the sun."

"You see any nets? Any fishing gear?"

Mikey glanced over at the old captain, and then at the empty *panga*, and shook his head. "He ain't got nothing in there but a jug of water."

"You see any reason for him to be out here in the middle of hot-as-shit nowhere?"

"I guess not."

"You guess? So you think it's possible that he motors all the way out here to take a nap 'cause he likes the smell of bat shit and mold and whatever else is growing inside that cave?"

Mikey shrugged.

"He's out here for a reason. I guarantee it."

"Maybe he's waiting for the divers to arrive," Mikey offered.

"Set the anchor, Einstein."

Zaragosa watched the young man drop the anchor and took quiet pride in the effectiveness of his double bluff. He'd taken shelter in the sea cave after a slow morning of keeping watch over the oyster bed. This was after taking Manolín to school and consulting with a few trusted amigos who planned to relieve him later that afternoon, after the first restful night since the accident. All because of the rich gringo and his generosity. The goateed man in the fish-skin cap had given him a large advance on a promised continuing windfall.

Zaragosa knew that realizing that windfall would depend on many factors. These included the truthfulness of the gringo to keep his promise, the health of the oyster bed, the protection of the secret. Much of it was beyond Zaragosa's control, and so he hid the American money in a sack of pinto beans kept in the corner of the shack, and when the sun came up, walked Manolín to the one-room classroom before heading out to the island. After a heartfelt send-off to his fellow *pangeros,* who headed straight for their usual fishing grounds.

All morning, Zaragosa had purposefully stayed hundreds of meters from the oyster bed in case a boat did show up, but by midday nobody had arrived and Zaragosa needed a break from the heat. He pulled into the sea cave for a short siesta. An hour later he heard the boat approaching, but he didn't move until they were directly on him. He acted casual to avoid any suspicion that he was concerned, even when he noticed the forest of scuba tanks lashed to the stern rail of the sailboat.

He knew immediately why the two men had sailed so far from La Paz with so much gear. It had not been to gaze at fish or hunt lobster. Isla San Jose was no better than Espíritu Santo for that, and Espíritu Santo was much closer to the marinas. Recreational divers who traveled this far always veered farther offshore for the famed underwater boulders of Las Animas, where enormous schools of fish swarmed just beneath the clean, clear deep waters.

No, these two men were here for something more valuable than memories and *langosta.* The pale-faced man was too aggressive to be a recreational diver. Zaragosa understood little English, but his senses at sea were keen and he quickly catalogued the probabilities. Which was why he'd told them to leave. Told them the diving here was poor. Because he wanted them to remain right here. Far from the oyster bed. He wanted them to drain their tanks of air and return to La Paz with nothing more than frustration and a sunburn. The two strangers could dive the area around the sea cave forever and not find a single oyster.

"*Buena suerte,*" Zaragosa said to the young man at the bow of the sailboat. Then he one-armed the small anchor into the *panga.*

"Okay," Mikey said, dropping the much larger anchor overboard. "*Gracias* and *vaya con Dios.*"

Zaragosa yanked the starter cord on the outboard engine and motored away from the sailboat, and then away from the oyster bed, hidden in thirty feet of water almost a quarter of a mile to the north in the opposite direction, safe for the moment from the two men with greed in their eyes.

CHAPTER THIRTY-FIVE

Isla San Jose, Baja California Sur

Tawny and Roscoe spent the early morning making love, exploring the rocky terrain of the desert island, and snacking on their supply of tortillas and mangoes. As the sun began to warm the hillside, they spotted the old fisherman and his *panga* and noticed that the boy was missing. They watched as the old man lingered off in the distance, hugging the shoreline near a large sea cave. For two hours he drifted about before finally pulling into the cave and out of sight.

"This stakeout stuff sucks," Roscoe said, rolling up his sleeping bag and preparing for the trek back to their skiff hidden on the lee-side shore.

"Something's brewing," Tawny said without lowering the binoculars.

"Yeah, my need for cooked food and cold beer."

Tawny lowered the binoculars. "You remember that sailboat anchored off the bar? The one with the crooked mast?"

"Not really."

"Well, it's here."

Roscoe dropped his sleeping bag to the rocks. "No way."

"Way." She handed him the glasses.

"What are the odds that two boats from San Carlos end up right here?" he asked her.

"Long."

He handed back the binoculars. "So you don't think it's a coincidence?"

"Nope."

"Some random gringo in a crappy sailboat just happens to know about the pearls?"

"Seems impossible, I know." She settled into the shadow of a large boulder and watched the sailboat approach the sea cave.

"So we wait?"

"We wait."

Roscoe sighed heavily and sat on his rolled sleeping bag. "I'm not spending another night up here."

An hour later they watched the sailboat drop anchor after a short exchange with the old man. Then they watched the old man pull anchor and motor off toward the south end of the island. Within minutes one of the two men on the sailboat suited up in scuba gear and dropped over the transom.

"I don't get it," Roscoe said, yanking his cap from his head and wiping sweat from his face. "It's like some weird conspiracy, and we're the dupes."

"Except the reef is way over here," Tawny said, pointing to the dark swath of water between their hideout and the sea cave. "If those guys are in on it, why are they diving so far away from the oysters?"

"Maybe a second oyster bed?"

"Maybe."

Roscoe cursed. "Which means more waiting and watching, right?"

"Right."

CHAPTER THIRTY-SIX

La Paz, Baja California Sur

Fish felt the phone vibrate with the incoming text and quickly finished banding a set of hundreds. He looked at the screen and scowled. Then he shook his head and handed the phone to Toozie.

"The photo of Skegs," he said darkly.

"What do you think his other side looks like?" she asked, and handed back the phone.

"Not good."

"Call them and set up the drop."

"Last time they sent a local boy."

"No one else can be involved. Tell them you'll leave it in an empty beer carton out by the trash bins in the parking lot of the marina. Tell them you'll return to the helm so they can see you aren't planning to attack or follow them."

Fish hit *redial* and put the phone on *speaker*.

"Better be important," came a voice Fish didn't recognize.

"Put Skegs on the phone."

"Who?"

"The guy you roughed up. That was an amateur move sending me his profile. He better be alive."

"Taking the profile shot wasn't my idea. I'd have shown you the full handiwork. Show you we're serious."

"Put Skegs on the phone now!"

"Here's the new plan. Ransom's doubled. I'm sending a man to your boat. You call me when he gets there. I'll put you on *speaker* so you can know your pal's alive. Once you hand over the cash,

I cut him loose. But"—the man made a satisfied sound with his throat—"you try to follow the cash and we put a knife in his back. *Comprende?*"

"I don't give a shit about the money."

The phone went dead.

Fish turned to Toozie. "That was definitely *not* the big guy I took out with the cactus arm."

"I thought you dunked him in a shark cage."

"We did, but that was *after* the cactus lesson."

Toozie raised her eyebrows with anticipation.

"Sounds worse than it was."

"So who's the new guy?"

"No idea, but he sounded more serious than the others. And a hell of a lot more sober."

"He's also demanding way more than the extra ten grand the other guys wanted yesterday?"

Fish nodded. "Double."

"Something's not right."

Fish retrieved the army surplus bag and counted out an extra ten grand, quickly bundling them into two stacks of fifty. He added the new stacks to the other two and said, "They're not planning to release Skegs, are they?"

"I'd like to borrow a gun."

This time it was Fish who raised his brow.

"I couldn't exactly smuggle mine down on the plane. You know, customs and everything."

"As a nonresident, it would be illegal for me to have a gun down here."

"I'm in a bit of a hurry."

"Up top. Starboard puka, just under the captain's seat."

"Puka?"

"Hawaiian word. Means a hiding place or a compartment. At least that's what Skegs thinks."

"I thought Skegs was a Seri Indian."

"I have my doubts."

Toozie hurried up the helm ladder. "Is it loaded?" she asked without looking back.

"Yep. And the safety's on."

Moments later Toozie returned to the back deck. "Okay, I want you to call me the minute the pickup leaves with the money."

"You're leaving already?"

"Rental car's in the lot. I've got to move it a few blocks and then wait for the signal. Find out where these morons are holed up."

"Not without me."

Toozie shook her head. "I've tailed a few bad guys over the years. And candidly, you'd be a distraction." She saw his face drop. "Not in a bad way," she quickly added, "but I need to focus if we want Skegs back alive."

"Except we're not talking about one bad guy. We're talking at least four now. And three of them are fighters. Thugs who burned down Cantina del Cielo."

"Just my type."

"I'm serious, Toozie."

"You're also emotionally connected. That can lead to problems."

Fish flexed his wide shoulders. "I'd feel better if we stayed together."

Toozie reached out and touched him on the arm. "I just need to see where they're keeping Skegs. Get the lay of the land before we decide what to do. In all these years of chasing bad guys, my safety net has always been information and patience." She gave a confident smile. "Trust me, Francis," she said, using his given name. "I want Skegs back alive *and* our thirty grand."

"*Our* thirty grand."

"You know what I mean."

"I don't care about the money."

"I know you don't." She threw her leg over the gunwale as if she were mounting a horse, and then hopped to the dock and hurried past the boats toward the rental car in the parking lot.

❦ ❦ ❦

Jimbo stumbled out of the cab and waited for a boat owner to pass through the locked gate before barging through it and down the main dock where the *Fish Goddess* was tied off near the fuel pumps.

It was midafternoon, and the sun's rays bounced off the water like blades of steel. Jimbo hardly noticed. In one hand he carried an old Trader Joe's cloth bag that Kraken had scrounged from the trunk of the Buick. In the other hand he held a can of Modelo Light. He finished the beer as he walked and then pitched it into the marina.

"Howdy, asshole," he said to the broad-shouldered man standing on the back deck of the trawler. "Remember me?"

"How could I forget a classy guy like you?" Fish said. He reached down and loosened the safety tie on the machete strapped to his thigh.

"That supposed to scare me?"

"I don't much care if it does."

"You got the money?"

"First we make the call." Fish dug into his zipper pocket for the phone.

"Not until I count the dough."

Fish glared at the man. Did he live every moment of his life drunk?

"Toss the money, tough guy," the man said. "I want to see it and feel it. Then you can make your stupid call."

"What's to stop you from running?"

"A twelve-pack for lunch." Jimbo laughed at the joke.

Fish didn't. He watched the man sway in the sun, then slowly backed to the saloon door and disappeared belowdecks. Moments later he emerged with a small cooler.

"You're offering me more beer?" Jimbo asked with a grin.

"Start counting." Fish tossed the cooler.

Jimbo nearly listed over as he caught it, but he kept his feet. He set it to the dock and swiveled open the top. Four neat stacks of banded hundred-dollar bills sat among bags of fish jerky. Jimbo thumbed through the money and then glanced around the dock. Satisfied nobody was watching, he transferred the cash to the Trader Joe's bag and snapped closed the cooler. He stood and lobbed it to the back deck, where it bounced off the tarp and crashed to the varnished teakwood.

"What's under the tarp?"

"Cops."

Jimbo stood suddenly and again nearly fell into the water.

"Or maybe it's a submarine with titanium rotors."

"That wasn't funny."

"Neither's the little game you and your buddies are playing. Who's the new guy?"

"What new guy?" he asked, unable to mask his surprise. Jimbo hadn't expected the man to know about Kraken.

"The one who's sober and threatened to knife Skegs in the back."

"Tank's not feeling good, so we added a man," Jimbo lied.

"I've played fair so far, but any of you losers lay another hand on Skegs and I switch to dirty." He narrowed his glare. "You do not want to call my bluff."

Jimbo took a shaky step back, away from the side of the boat. "How much is in each bundle?"

"Five thousand."

"Boss said he ain't going to release your buddy until he sees the money."

Fish pocketed the phone. "Then let him see it."

"You ain't shorting us, right?"

Almost in a single motion, Fish hopped the gunwale and grabbed Jimbo by the neck. "You have thirty minutes to release Skegs. No more time. No more bullshit. You got it, Mr. Jimmy?"

"How'd you know my name?" Jimbo croaked, trying to glare at him.

Fish released him. "I know everything about you. Now get the hell out of my sight before I do something stupid." Fish pommel-horsed back into the boat.

Jimbo regained his composure. "You're lucky my hands are full of cash."

Fish fought the urge to leap back to the dock and fling the fighter into the water. Instead, he placed a call and pressed *speaker*.

"We got a problem?" came the sober voice of the new guy.

"You're pal Jimmy here says you want to see the money before you release Skegs."

"Good to know the beer hasn't clouded his memory."

"That wasn't our deal."

"Thing is, I don't trust these idiots. I'm sure you understand."

"So now I'm supposed to trust you."

"Seems unfair, but that's the way these things work out sometimes."

"You've done this sort of thing before?"

"Let's just say I know what I'm doing."

"How do I know he's even alive?"

Fish heard a scuffling sound, and then the voice he'd been waiting for said, "Meet me at my favorite bar on the boardwalk. If I'm not there in thirty minutes, unleash the wolves on these parasites."

Fish smiled.

"Clock starts now," Fish said, and hung up the phone. He turned to Jimbo. "You'll never get away with it, you know."

"We'll see."

"It's not too late to fix this."

"You should do stand-up."

"Time's running out."

Jimbo conjured up a defiant scowl. "You and I ain't finished."

"Until next time then," Fish said, and tipped his hat with an easy grin. He turned and strolled into the saloon for his sunglasses. When he returned, the kidnapper was gone. He quickly dialed his phone.

"We good?" came Toozie's voice.

"Change of plan."

There was a pause and Fish said, "Drive over to the Estrella Bar. It's a few blocks away on the *malecón*."

"What? Why?"

"Skegs said he'd be there in thirty minutes. I'll be there in five. We need to get his take on the new guy before we go in all guns ablazing."

"You keep this up, and you might just lose that reputation for recklessness."

"Information and patience, right?"

"There's hope for you after all."

Fish pocketed the phone, leaped over the railing, and hit the dock in a full barefoot sprint, the sheathed machete unstrapped and clutched in his hand.

CHAPTER THIRTY-SEVEN

La Paz, Baja California Sur

Kraken worked fast. He knew Jimbo would arrive in fifteen to twenty minutes. More than enough time to teach the big man with the infected scalp a lesson in how to take orders.

Kraken hustled to the half-dozen scuba tanks stacked upright in the corner of the apartment. All were purchased secondhand, their aluminum surfaces dented from misuse, the old coats of white paint chipped and rusty. Skegs hefted the closest twenty-pound cylinder over his shoulder and carried it to the bed where Tank lay passed out on his back, arms splayed out. The fighter's head glowed like a fireplug and gleamed with sweat and raw-looking sores oozing a bloody yellow discharge. Kraken laid the tank on the bed beside the snoring man and retrieved the roll of duct tape from the kitchen sink. Nearly half remained after securing their hostage's legs and arms to the lawn chair and then the chair to the leg of the bed.

"I don't know exactly what you're up to, but it ought to be good," Skegs said from across the room, sitting up straighter and tugging surreptitiously on his sticky binds. "Got any popcorn?"

Kraken ignored him and gently set the tank of compressed air into position snug to Tank's side, the valve end atop his near shoulder. He lifted the other limp arm and pulled the heavy man over toward him, onto his side and into an embrace of the aluminum cylinder. Once he had him settled, he rotated the tank so that the pressure valve was aimed directly into the unconscious man's open mouth, then freed a length of duct tape and began winding it around Tank's body, his arms, and the belly of the compressed air. By the time Tank stirred, Kraken had encircled his victim a dozen or more times, pinning the scuba tank to his chest and arms.

As if finally beginning to sense what was happening to him, Tank let out a sudden groan and kicked with his legs, but still didn't awaken. Kraken watched him settle, then freed another length of tape from the roll and, taking it between his teeth, rolled Tank onto his back again and hopped atop him, straddling cylinder and man. Tank's eyes flew open, and he gave a senseless bark as Kraken hoisted his head off the pillow by his hair, wrapped a quick turn around the back of the infected head, and cinched the pressure valve deep into his gaping mouth. With Tank bucking wild-eyed beneath him, Kraken wound the tape around the head and valve a half-dozen times, looking like a rodeo cowboy finishing off a roped calf. Tank thrashed and rocked beneath him, bloodshot eyes blinking and rolling. He tried to knee his captor but only managed to crack it brutally against the solid base of the scuba tank, which in turn wrought untold dental havoc as the tank's valve rattled savagely about in his mouth. His wide eyes went blind in pain.

"Righteous!" Skegs hollered.

As Tank came to just a little, his eyes rolled to the mescal salesman.

Skegs lifted his middle finger to him. "Paybacks are a bitch, right?"

Kraken turned to Skegs and sighed. "Do I need to use the rest of the duct tape on you?"

"Sorry, boss." Skegs lowered his finger. "Carry on, my man."

Kraken returned his attention to Tank, beneath him on the bed. "So here's the new plan, tough guy," he said, dismounting him and brushing back a greasy lock of hair. "Your drunk dumbass partner will be here in a few minutes with another twenty grand. My twenty grand. Which will go nicely with *this* ten grand," he said, pointing down to Tank's thigh, where the first installment of ransom money was still taped.

Again Tank flopped like a boated tuna as he fought to free himself. Kraken watched until it ceased to amuse him, then stepped to him and opened the valve. Tank's molten eyes bulged, and his cheeks puffed out like balloons. His chest cavity expanded, and his stomach bloated with air and pressed the heavy cylinder against Kraken's thighs. A thin whistle escaped Tank's nostrils, and he stiffened with pain, clamping his eyes tightly. Kraken shut off the valve.

"You do not want to fuck with me," he told the fighter.

Tank's cheeks deflated as the air leaked from the seal of tape around his mouth. He drew fast breaths through his nose and nodded, his watery eyes opening and closing in relief.

Kraken reached down again and began to tear away the tape holding the ransom money to Tank's thigh. Forgetting his promise to cooperate just that quickly, Tank released a muffled howl into his mouthpiece and arched his back as if electrified. His face grew purple with exertion as he yanked at his binds and bucked against the scuba tank. Sucking great gulps of air through his nose and screaming muffled profanities into the valve, he actually seemed to be making some headway in freeing his legs from the tank. Kraken remounted him, this time facing away from him, and went to work resecuring Tank's legs to the scuba tank. Tank double-bucked, sending Kraken bouncing against the wall and onto the floor. Enraged, Kraken scrambled to his feet, lunged for the valve's fat handle, and wrenched it open with a hard twist of his wrist. A muffled pop sounded in the room.

"Holy fuck!" Skegs said, making a choking sound and jerking hard against the lawn chair.

Kraken regained his composure and glanced down at the mutilated face of his hostage. Tank's exploded cheeks resembled a shock of crimson confetti. Blood-colored mucus oozed from the dead man's nostrils. His lips were shredded ribbons of red spittle. His bulging eyes stared at the ceiling in a confused web of scarlet.

"Dumb son of a bitch," Kraken muttered, wiping the wet spray of blood from his face. He reached down and yanked the bag of money from Tank's leg. Then he turned to Skegs. "Don't you say a fucking word or you're next."

Skegs nodded without looking at the mess on the bed.

Kraken tossed the money into the sink. He grabbed the remaining turns of duct tape from the bed and went to Skegs.

"On second thought, I can't take any chances," he said, and used the last of the tape to cover Skegs's mouth.

He went to the small closet and rummaged through the pile of dirty clothes and old shoes and broken fishing reels until he found what he needed. He kneeled to the old tackle box and opened its winged top. Moments later he was busily threading a length of heavy monofilament fishing line through the metal eyelets of a handful of torpedo weights. He tripled the line into a foot-long dropper loop and felt the weight dangle from his grip. He swung his arm easily toward the floor and watched the homemade slapjack smash a dent into the linoleum. Kraken grinned maliciously.

Then he stood, surveyed the room with satisfaction, took his position behind the front door, and waited.

CHAPTER THIRTY-EIGHT

Isla San Jose, Baja California Sur

Angus Black surfaced from his third dive in as many hours. At first he was worried about his last-minute deckhand, Mikey, sniffing around the boat for valuables while he was underwater. The cache of cell phones and wallets and jewelry, he was less worried about. That he could explain. Petty theft was the universal language with guys like Mikey. But a pearl would be trickier to explain. Which was why he'd long ago tossed the yellow plastic bag into the ocean. The pearl he had moved hours ago from the drawer near his master berth to the soap dish in the head. He mixed it into a handful of sea glass, camouflaging it like some common marble. If he'd learned anything from all those years of breaking and entering, it was to hide valuables in plain sight. Gems cloaked in the verisimilitudes of everyday life provided invisibility to all but the caretaker.

Angus turned to his back and kicked his flippers toward the boat. A light wind had finally risen and ruffled the surface of the afternoon sea. As he neared the trailing rope tied to the stern cleat, he noticed the fleet of *pangas* approaching on the horizon. He doubled his effort and soon climbed aboard the stolen sailboat.

"We've got visitors," Mikey announced, turning from the oncoming *panga* flotilla to watch the Canadian slip from his scuba gear. He knew the man wasn't an albino, but damn, that was some white skin.

"I see them," Angus said, quickly drying off and applying sunscreen before slipping into sweatpants and a long-sleeved shirt. He ducked belowdecks and emerged moments later wearing a wide-brimmed hat—and a pistol tucked into his waistband with its handle exposed.

"Whoa," Mikey said nervously. "What's with the firepower?"

"It's the old guy again. He's brought reinforcements. I like to have insurance in these situations."

"What situation? They're fishermen. This is probably their fishing ground."

Angus turned from Mikey and watched the half-dozen *pangas* slow within shouting distance. Each boat carried two men in blood-streaked overalls. None was smiling. Most were taut with muscle from hauling nets filled with fish. A few wore gray beards flecked in fish scales, their beer bellies prominent beneath their equally gray sweatshirts.

"*Señor*," Zaragosa called out. "*No buceo aquí.*"

Angus turned to Mikey. "What's he want now?"

"He says you can't dive here."

"Why the hell not?"

Mikey stepped to the gunwale nearest the fishermen and asked for the reason.

"*Este agua es sagrada.*"

Mikey turned to Angus. "This water is sacred."

"All of it?"

Zaragosa pointed at the cave. "*La Cueva.*"

Mikey started to translate, when Angus patted the butt of the gun at his waist. "Yeah, the cave. I got it." He leaned menacingly over the gunwale and said, "No fucking oysters here anyway. Get the hell out of our way. We're trying a new spot."

"We are?" Mikey asked.

Angus kept his eyes on Zaragosa and said, "Pull the anchor, deckhand. We're moving through these assholes. They tried to intimidate us into moving the other direction. Goddamn amateurs."

Mikey nodded to the *pangeros* and then apologized in Spanish, explaining that they were moving to a new spot. He also mentioned his distrust of the boat owner and said the gun had come as a surprise to him.

"What the fuck was all that about?" Angus asked, finally turning away from the *pangeros* and facing Mikey.

"Just being friendly so they'll leave us alone," Mikey lied, and hustled up to the bow to pull anchor.

CHAPTER THIRTY-NINE

La Paz, Baja California Sur

Jimbo nearly skipped into the studio apartment. "Cha-*ching*!" he hollered happily, the money bag held in his outstretched hands. "Like taking candy from a retard."

The room was silent. Jimbo blinked away the buzz of the *ballena* bottle of beer he'd purchased on his cab ride back to the apartment. Tank lay faceup on the bed, a scuba tank taped to his chest and mouth, his face a vast pulp of skin and blood. His bald head was chalky instead of fire-ant-red with infection, and the forest of welts covering his scalp seemed less swollen, almost deflated.

"Yo, Tank!" he yelled, leaping to the side of the bed and ignoring Skegs, who sat wide-eyed in the lawn chair. "What the fuck happened, man?"

He remembered the dive shop owner and whipped around with hatred in his booze-flushed face, but Kraken had already begun his swing of the leaded fishing weights, which met Jimbo's left temple with a sodden crunch. He toppled face-first to the linoleum floor, his forehead bouncing with a second, louder crack. Blood immediately began to pool around his scalp.

"Talk about a retard," Kraken commented, his mismatched eyes dancing. He bent down and retrieved the bag of money from Jimbo's lifeless hand, then returned to the closet and lifted a moth-eaten T-shirt from the pile of clothes and began wiping down the room. "In case the authorities get wind of the stink before I get back from my favorite island."

Skegs yelled into his taped mouth and jerked at his binds, feeling something give way in the aluminum armrests.

"Relax, cowboy. I'm not leaving you here. You won't like where I'm taking you, but it'll be safer"—he glanced at the two dead bodies—"and a lot less bloody."

Skegs yelled again, but Kraken just smiled.

"Don't waste your breath. Nobody can hear you. And in a couple of hours it'll be dark and no one will see you, either, when I move you to the trunk of the Buick."

Skegs bellowed into the tape.

Kraken laughed. "No need for profanity, if that's what that was. You're mumbling, buddy! Anyway, no worries: It's a big trunk. Plenty of room for you and that lawn chair. Safekeeping while I head to everybody's favorite island for a well-deserved payday."

Then he sidestepped the blood on the linoleum floor and poured himself a glass of water from the kitchen sink. He downed it, sighed with satisfaction, and then spent the rest of the afternoon meticulously erasing all signs of his appearance at the apartment. At nightfall, he was in the old Buick heading for the old man's boat with Skegs and the lawn chair folded into the trunk.

Kraken planned to ditch the old car and take the old man's boat to Espíritu Santo for a few hours until the rich guy dropped one last ten-grand goody-bag on the beach. Then, if the money added up, he might truthfully divulge the hostage's whereabouts. Then again, someone was bound to get curious and inspect the abandoned car. They would either hear the weak cries of the dehydrated prisoner or smell the body rotting in the humidity. One thing, however, Kraken knew for certain.

Forty large was a hell of a bankroll for a long-overdue fiesta in Cabo San Lucas.

CHAPTER FORTY

La Paz, Baja California Sur

Fish entered the Estrella Bar, gleaming with sweat. It took a long moment for his eyes to adjust to the fluorescence of the bar after his five-minute jog directly into the late-afternoon sun. The bartender spotted him over the crowd of sunburned fishermen raucously bragging about the ones that got away. She waved.

Fish threaded the horde of potbellies and ordered a Fresca.

"So where's the love of my life?" she asked as she placed the soda on the bar top. Her jeans and the cartoon sharks covering her torn T-shirt had collected mixer stains since Fish had last seen her hours earlier, but her smile remained warm, her bronze eyes delighted to see him.

"*He's* the love of your life? I thought you liked the goatee?"

"Oh, I do, honey," the bartender said with a wink, then whisked down the bar, pouring shots of tequila with the deftness of a circus performer.

Fish watched her go and smiled at the show, feeling more relaxed than he had in days. Toozie was here, and Skegs was about to walk in and complain about the amount of time it took to free him. Probably lament the paltry ransom required to spring a man of his renown.

Fish drank the cold Fresca and felt the sweat beginning to cool on his skin. Laughter erupted behind him and when he turned, he saw one of the fishermen extending his arms wide as if measuring the girth of the lost marlin. As he started to swivel back to the bar, he saw Toozie coming up the sidewalk. A smile spilled across his face.

She paused at the doorway, and Fish stared longingly. The low-lying sun highlighted the natural reds of her hair, its long twists, dropping past her shoulders, held in a loose ponytail. She wore a simple silver necklace with a turquoise pendant. Below that were a teal blouse and loose-fitting jeans. A pair of dark brown cowboy boots added an inch to her already tall stature. A hand-sewn cloth bag covered in colorful desert flowers hung from her shoulder.

Toozie entered the bar, pushed her sunglasses atop her head, and scanned the room. Fish stood, and even in bare feet towered above the other patrons. Toozie caught his eye and hurried through the crowd.

"Skegs should be on his way," she said. "Tracking devices showed a short stop not far from here. But now they're on the move. Heading toward Pichilingue fast." She reached into her bag and removed the GPS-like device. "I'd say they're in a car, but it doesn't make sense for them to be heading in that direction. The road dead-ends not far from there."

"Tecolote Beach," Fish agreed.

"Tecolote Beachfront Estates," Toozie reminded him, and reached for his Fresca.

"I'd rather remember its heyday." He watched her take a drink of his soda. "Want me to order you something?"

"Nope. Just wanted a sip. The celebratory Negra Modelo is awaiting Skegs's arrival." She held the GPS up to get a better signal.

"You giving out your secret spots?" one of the fishermen called out. He reached into the zipper pocket of his baggy shorts and raised his own handheld GPS. "Trade you a few of mine." He started punching buttons.

"Maybe some other time," Toozie said kindly.

"Bet you don't have Wahoo Reef in there," he assured her. "Here, type this setting."

He'd started to call out the numbers, when Fish stood and announced loudly, "Next round's on me."

The fisherman swallowed the remaining numbers and rushed the bar with the other happy gringos.

"Nice one," Toozie said. She glanced at the tracking device and frowned. "They stopped near the ferry terminal."

"Escaping to the mainland?" Fish asked.

"That would have been my first guess."

"But?"

"But they went the opposite direction."

Fish waited as she frowned.

"They're heading out to sea."

Fish started to respond, when his cell phone vibrated against his thigh. He pulled it from the pocket of his sailcloth pants and eyed the incoming call. "Uh-oh," he said, and raced outside to escape the noise of the bar.

Toozie joined him just as he pocketed the phone.

"Trouble?" she asked.

"They're demanding a final ten. Espíritu Santo. Midnight tonight. The inside of the isthmus connecting it to Isla Partida."

"Skegs?" she asked haltingly.

"Says we get him when we deliver the ten to the beach without cops."

"What did you say?"

"I said no cops."

      ❧ ❧ ❧

Fish and Toozie made it to Marina de La Paz in record time and climbed aboard the *Fish Goddess*. They shoved off, ignored the no-wake rule, and were soon planing across the open ocean. The night sky carried a light breeze, and overhead an audience of stars applauded their approach to Espíritu Santo.

"Kidnappers are hiding on the other side of the island," Toozie said, reading the handheld tracking instrument.

"The isthmus has a shallow bay on the inside and a deep bay on the outside."

"They're sitting close to shore in the deep bay. At least, that's where the money is."

"Makes sense," Fish said, adjusting the trim tabs to pull extra speed from the twin Caterpillar engines. "He wants me to drop the money on the inside. Which would mean anchoring and taking the dinghy through the shallows to the beach."

Toozie looked out at the massive island silhouetted in the night. "While one of them waits in the dark to grab the money before you can get back to the boat."

"Exactly."

"They'll have quite a head start with us on the wrong side of the island. It's got to be at least a mile long."

"At least." He angled away from the shallow side of the island.

"What are you doing?"

"Changing the rules."

"You think it's another ruse?"

"I think it's time we saved Skegs."

"And if they're armed?"

"They're not expecting us. They have no idea that we know where they are. After we hit them, they'll be lucky to retrieve a weapon before it sinks to the seafloor."

Toozie's mouth screwed into a question mark. "Hit them how?"

"This old trawler is steel-hulled. Its prow is high and hard as a chisel. They don't have a chance."

"You're planning to ram them?" She paused, thoughtful. "And if Skegs is aboard?"

"He better be aboard."

"But—"

"He'll be held in a bunkroom or the helm where they can keep an eye on him. I'm taking out their stern. By the time they realize what happened, I'll be aboard. The boat will be sinking. They'll be in survivor mode. The last thing they'll want is Skegs."

"Well . . ." Her eyes crinkled at the corners. "I hate to admit it, but that's the best crazy idea I've heard in a long time."

"Really?" Fish asked, looking honestly shocked. "I was sure you'd hate it after our last two experiences with bad guys."

"These guys are a different breed. You've given them more than enough chances to take the money and run. That makes them dumber or meaner than your usual criminal. A surprise attack might just be the perfect defense against another broken promise."

Fish took a hand off the nautical wheel and pulled her into a one-armed hug.

"I'm glad you're here."

"Me, too," she said, squeezing him gently. "And just in case your cautious recklessness doesn't work, I plan to keep this handy." She held his gun up in the starlight and grinned. "In case one of our bozos tries to board us while you're rescuing Skegs from his near drowning."

He placed his hand back to the wheel. "I like your forward planning. And for what it's worth, Skegs is a hell of a swimmer."

CHAPTER FORTY-ONE

La Paz, Baja California Sur

It took Skegs an hour to break free of the lawn chair in the trunk of the parked car. It was dark, and the skin of his wrists and ankles was raw and bruised from banging into the exposed metal hinges and the struggle with the duct tape. His forearm ached from a cut caused by a piece of twisted aluminum that had split during the struggle. He was also soaked with sweat and beginning to dehydrate. The trunk was hot and cramped and deafeningly loud with his desperate attempts to kick open the locked hatch. It was so loud that he hadn't heard the approaching footfalls until he caught the sound of metal crunching against the lip of the trunk.

Skegs quickly found his back and bent his knees painfully to his chest, his broken huaraches flat to the underside of the trunk. A second crunch of metal and Skegs kicked out with all of his waning strength. The trunk flew open and Skegs thrust out his fists, expecting a fight. Instead, he stared unsteadily into the eyes of an old Mexican shrimper holding a small hand gaff in a defensive posture. The old man stepped away from him, bent to the graveled lot, and used the gaff to scoop the handle of a plastic jug of water, which he handed to Skegs. While Skegs painfully sat upright and slaked his thirst, the old shrimper turned and walked toward the small dock where a skiff lay tied to a cleat.

"*Oye,*" Skegs called out after draining nearly the entire jug of water.

The old man turned.

"*Gracias.*"

The man nodded, then stepped to the dock and untied the skiff.

"If it's not too much trouble," Skegs said in Spanish, crawling from the trunk and loping toward him with an awkward gait, his arm cradling his broken ribs, "I could use a ride to Marina de La Paz."

The man looked him over. "You've got a car." He wagged a crooked finger at the Buick.

"It's not mine."

"Drogas son muy malas."

"Do I look like a drug dealer to you?"

The man's nod was slight, but unmistakable.

Skegs scanned his bloody forearm and torn board shorts and noted the wrecked state of his blue AFTCO fishing shirt, the printed game fish grimed with filth and blood and dried vomit. He gingerly touched his swollen eye. "Drug dealers kill their victims. I'm still alive."

"For now."

"My best friend is a rich gringo," Skegs said, taking short breaths to alleviate the ache at his rib cage. "The man who did this to me is also a gringo. This is about ransom, not drugs."

"Buena suerte," the man said, and reached for the pull chord on the outboard engine.

"Wait," Skegs coughed painfully.

The man turned.

"What if I told you I was nabbed while attempting to conclude the Legend of Mechudo?"

The man's eyes widened.

"The pearls have been discovered. I will present the largest one to the church. But only if we hurry."

The old man's face softened, and he waved Skegs aboard. "As a boy I searched for the pearls," he said as Skegs settled himself. "Every day after school. Memories that are older than you." He crossed himself, a longing gaze to his old eyes. "I will take you to the marina."

Twenty minutes later they pulled into Marina de La Paz. The dock lights illuminated the plethora of sailboats and cruisers, but not the *Fish Goddess*. Skegs spotted the night watchman near the fuel dock watching a sea lion play with a dead yellowfin croaker.

Skegs asked the old man to motor to the fuel dock, where the guard met them with a wary gaze. Skegs explained in Spanish his connection to the *Fish Goddess*. The guard saw the bruises and the blood, and shook his head suspiciously.

"I got into a bar fight," Skegs lied.

The guard stood, unmoved.

"Macho Mescal?"

The guard's face betrayed recognition.

"I own the company," Skegs quickly added. "The owner of the *Fish Goddess* is one of my best customers. We registered the boat this morning. At dawn. His name is Atticus Fish, and he owns Cantina del Cielo in Puerto San Carlos."

The guard gave an assenting shrug of the shoulders. "I am sorry, amigo. That boat left over an hour ago. *El capitán* and a pretty señorita."

"Impossible," Skegs said, feeling his legs weaken. He dropped to one knee at the bow of the skiff and wrapped an arm around his ruined rib cage.

The guard waved them forward. "You need to see a doctor."

Skegs straightened. "I'll be okay." He turned to the old fisherman. "I know this looks bad, but—"

"I believe you, amigo."

The unexpected kindness of the stranger wobbled Skegs's legs once again, and he slumped back to the bow. He felt his heart pound and his eyes begin to mist. The day's difficulties suddenly rushed forward. The brutality of his kidnappers, the icy greed, and cold bloodlust of the dive shop owner. The vision of Tank's exploded face, and Jimbo's head lying in a pool of blood.

A hand touched Skegs's shoulder and he flinched. *"Me llamo* Santiago," the old man said, introducing himself. *"A dónde quiere ir?"*

Skegs sucked at the night air and cleared his mind. He wiped at the wetness beneath his good eye.

"Espíritu Santo," he said, remembering the dive shop owner's final words about the favorite island.

CHAPTER FORTY-TWO

Espíritu Santo, Baja California Sur

Thirty minutes after hitting open water, Fish pulled back on the throttles and entered the deepwater side of the isthmus. He could just make out the shadowy lines of the old wooden sportfisher anchored in the bay, close to shore. Its lights were off, but the heavy blanket of starlight gave it an eerie outline.

Fish checked his speed. Eight knots. He increased it to nine.

"Still sure about this?" Toozie asked. She stood beside him, bracing herself against the instrument panel.

"With a slight adjustment. Going to lessen the impact by clipping the corner of the transom just enough to bend the drive shaft and knock a hole in the hull. Plowing through the midsection brings the old diesel into play. That's a lot of heavy metal to crunch through. Could punch a hole in us."

"Or the people on board."

"Only one I'm worried about."

"You're not a killer, Francis," she said. "Let's do this right. Save Skegs *and* nab the bad guys. Even if they are dirtbags worthy of a burial at sea. Let somebody else play judge and jury for a change."

Fish agreed. "Good thing we have a portable jail cell under that tarp down on deck."

"Right," she said, remembering the shark cage.

"Thirty seconds to mayhem," Fish announced, and took direct aim at the corner stern of the dark boat.

Twenty feet from impact, a man appeared at the helm, waving frantically. Fish jammed the throttles full speed and felt the trawler rear up slightly as it cleaved through the soft planks of the stern. The old boat rocked heavily as water poured into the engine compartment and boiled up to the deck. Fish spun the trawler hard and came back alongside with a glancing blow to the gunwale and handed the controls to Toozie.

"Back away the instant I hit the deck," he instructed. "In case they try and board us." Then he raced from the helm and leaped to the watery deck of the sinking boat.

Toozie slammed the engines into reverse. She flipped on the deck light switches he'd shown her earlier, and a flood of halogens illuminated the surrounding water and wooden wreckage. She watched Fish duck into the saloon, and then caught sight of the man they'd seen earlier at the helm frantically waving them off. He stood now at the bow with a dry bag tucked beneath his arm. He glanced around once, then jumped into the water and started splashing toward shore.

Toozie engaged the anchor wench, and heard the chain rattle as it fed through the windlass and fell toward the sandy bottom. Then she raced from the helm to the bow of the trawler and dived into the warm sea after the man. He hadn't gotten far, with the dry bag held above his head while frantically paddling with his free arm. She caught up to him in the shallows as he struggled for a foothold, and looped an arm around his neck.

"You should have left the money behind," she said.

"Bitch," Kraken growled. He whipped the dry bag blindly at her head, keeping a grip on the handle.

Feeling the weight of twenty thousand dollars glance off her ear, Toozie tightened her forearm across Kraken's esophagus and slammed his face into the sea.

He bucked against her weight, but Toozie anticipated the move. She'd been raised on a ranch outside Tucson, Arizona, and had been breaking horses and ranging cattle since childhood. The ranch was hers now, and while it held less livestock, she still rode daily, and when she wasn't riding or working a case, she was fishing or hiking or swimming laps at the Y. Miles and miles of laps. Olympic laps. As a female P.I., fitness was as important as any firearm.

At the moment, however, her firearm was tucked inside her waistband filling with water, and so she hung on like a bull rider and waited for him to release the dry bag. It didn't take long. His free hand desperately grabbed her hair. Ignoring the pain, Toozie emptied her lungs and let her deadweight tire him. Kraken was a powerful man, though, and bucked free of her. She followed him to the surface, freeing her firearm as she went, and pistol-whipped him across the temple as he tried to swim away. Kraken went limp. Jamming her gun back into her waistband, Toozie hooked an arm around the unconscious kidnapper's throat and worked her way to shore with him.

As she dragged him up the pebbly beach, he began coughing violently. Before he could get his wits about him, she slipped the handle of the dry bag from where he'd snagged it in the crook of his arm and tossed it higher up the beach.

Kraken began to climb to his knees.

"No chance, asshole," she said, hefting a heavy beach stone and joining its weight to her own as she flattened him into the sand with a full-body press. "You even wiggle and I'll cave in the back of your head with this rock. You do not want to test me."

"Who the fuck are you?" Kraken croaked.

"Backup."

Loud splashing sounds filled the night air as Fish emerged from the water like an enraged Triton.

"Where is he, goddammit?!"

Toozie pushed away from Kraken and stood. "Skegs isn't on board?"

Fish jackhammered a knee into Kraken's back. "You son of a bitch. Where the hell is he?!"

"Fuck you," Kraken wheezed.

Fish looked up at Toozie, unable to mask the murderous intent in his eyes. "Get the dinghy."

CHAPTER FORTY-THREE

Marina de La Paz, Baja California Sur

Skegs explained the last few days to Santiago as they turned from the fuel dock and crossed the dark, calm water of the bay, moving from the initial confrontation with the UFC wannabes to the pale-faced man in the Cantina del Cielo fire to the dive shop encounter. Then he described the beatings, the crazy gringo demands, the dive shop owner, and the deaths of Tank and Jimbo.

"He said he was heading to everyone's favorite island," Skegs explained in Spanish as they zoomed from the bay into the night sea. "Everybody's favorite island is Espíritu Santo. The Holy Ghost with its long finger bays and hiking trails and friendly sea lions."

"And miles of empty shoreline for escaping with your friend's money and disappearing into the night?"

"I think so."

Santiago frowned. "Espíritu is a very big island to find a man hiding on a dark boat. He won't have his lights on."

"But Atticus will find him. I'm sure of it."

In the starlight Skegs could see the old captain smile and hear him say, "You could use some luck, amigo."

"Santiago," Skegs said, shielding his face from the spray of water feathering from the bow. "You are the luckiest thing that's happened to me in days."

An hour later they approached the island, and Santiago took the inside passage, searching every deep bay for his passenger's trawler. By midnight they'd found nothing but a few sailboats and a charter with a dozen kayakers partying around a bonfire.

"Not many places to hide on the ocean side," Santiago said matter-of-factly.

Skegs stared across the dark horizon bangled with starlight. "They have to be here. The other islands are too far away." Skegs's voice dropped. "Unless something has happened."

"We will keep searching then," Santiago said, and gunned the engine. Ten minutes later they rounded the point and saw the glow of bright deck lights in the distance.

"The isthmus!" Skegs said.

"Of course," Santiago agreed, and steered for the illuminated water.

❀ ❀ ❀

Fish worked the hydraulic controls and raised the shark cage from the water. Kraken emerged gasping for air. His clothes were torn from his struggle with Toozie and repeated attempts to break through the bars of the cage. He was also shivering with exhaustion and the loss of body heat. Still, his mismatched eyes held more disdain than fear, the knife scars on his face like waxy bits of rope in the bright deck lights.

"I'll take the dinghy *and* the money." He coughed. "Handheld radio so when I'm safely away from you and your female piranha over there, I can radio back and tell you where he's at."

"Your credibility is more than a little suspect at this point," Fish said. "What happened to the fighters?"

"Who?"

Fish started to lower the cage.

"You kill me and you'll never find him."

"For all I know, he's dead."

"He's alive."

"Where?"

Kraken flashed a defiant grin.

Fish sent the cage into the water.

Toozie stepped to his side and said, "It's not working. Pull him up. We can head back and threaten to turn him into the police. He'll spill it then. Mexican jails are highly motivating."

Fish was about to agree, when they heard the sound of an outboard engine roaring toward them from the blackness. Fish hurried to the stern, shading his eyes from the bright deck lights.

"Get the gun," he called out.

"The fighters?" Toozie asked as she retrieved the pistol from the helm.

"I'd bet on it," Fish said, then backed to the tarped submarine and waited.

Toozie crouched at the stern, the pistol aimed at the approaching boat. Moments later the skiff with Santiago and Skegs zoomed into the pool of light surrounding the trawler.

"Got any beer on board?" Skegs called out, momentarily forgetting his sore ribs. "Preferably one that's cold, with a slice of *limón*."

Fish stood speechless.

"Skegs!" Toozie tucked the pistol to her waist and hurried to the deck.

"*Bueno,* sister sleuth."

Santiago cut the engine, and the skiff slid up against the dive step.

"About time you freed yourself from those idiots," Fish said, regaining his wits.

"Oh shit!" Toozie blurted, and raced to the hydraulic controls. "He's still down there."

Fish and Skegs and Santiago watched the shark cage rise heavily from the water.

Kraken writhed in a fetal position, his body covered with dozens of papaya-sized predators. He coughed out a lungful of water and tore at the web of tentacles covering his face.

"Holy fuck!" Skegs said as he painfully climbed aboard. "Humboldt squid. Little babies feasting on his sorry ass. Send him back down!"

"*Diablos rojos,*" Santiago said, and crossed himself.

As Toozie swung the cage aboard, a slew of squid dropped through the metal bars and splashed into the water, darting away like submersible missiles into the darkness. A few of the baby cephalopods, however, remained suctioned to Kraken's skin, their toothy tentacles gouging bloody rings into the dive shop owner's arms and legs, their parrotlike beaks pecking at the warm flesh. Kraken screamed as he tore at one clinging stubbornly to his temple. When he finally pulled it free, blood drained down his scarred sideburn.

Toozie wrenched open the cage door and entered. She kneeled to Kraken and pried the stubborn squids from his skin. Fish appeared at her side, clearing the juvenile predators from the cage and flipping them back into the water.

"He'll need a doctor," Toozie said, tossing the last squid overboard. "He's a mess."

Kraken groaned semiconsciously.

"Paybacks are a bitch!" Skegs yelled giddily. "Serves you right, motherfucker!"

Blood bubbled up from the forest of circular bite marks as Toozie sat him up. "I need a towel and some water."

"Not a chance," Skegs said defiantly.

Kraken slumped against the bars of the cage and vomited.

Skegs kicked him in the thigh, and then doubled over in pain. Santiago appeared with a threadbare Mexican blanket and laid it across Skegs's shoulders.

Fish gave an appreciative nod to the stranger, hurried into the saloon, and returned with a handful of towels and a jug of water. "The lights must have attracted the school of squid," he said, handing the water to Toozie. "He would have died if you hadn't remembered him down there."

"He still might," she said, and held the jug to Kraken's lips. Then she set about gently washing his multitude of wounds.

CHAPTER FORTY-FOUR

Isla San Jose, Baja California Sur

At dawn, Mikey rose and quietly moved from the back of the sailboat toward the foredeck, tiptoeing past the portside window where the owner slept. Bored out of his mind, he'd dozed off on his night watch, when a noise stirred him from his sleep. Now, as his eyes adjusted to the early-morning light, he spotted the cluster of *pangas* that remained anchored between their sailboat and the sacred sea cave. Beyond that he saw the source of the new noise. A trawler had dropped anchor about half a mile down the shoreline, equidistant from the cave. He'd wandered back to the stern, when the saloon door flung open and Angus Black stomped out, wearing his wet suit.

"Your friends still keeping us company?" he growled.

"They're not my friends."

Angus screwed his lips into a doubtful sneer. "You fill the tanks like I asked?"

"All ten are ready to go."

Angus pushed past his deckhand and checked the scuba tank strapped to his dive vest. He gave a satisfied grunt and secured the vest around his chest.

"How about I give it a try?" Mikey asked as Angus hefted a pair of swim fins and mask from the starboard rack and unlatched the stern railing. "I'm getting bored up here."

Angus slipped on the fins and backed through the opening. He spit loudly into the mask and spread the natural defogger across the faceplate.

"I'm a pretty good swimmer," Mikey continued as the Canadian bent to the waterline and dipped the mask and cleaned the faceplate. "Four eyes are better than two."

Angus thought about his untrusted deckhand snooping on board while the local fishermen hovered around. He splashed into the sea and slid the mask over his face. Before placing the regulator into his mouth, he craned his neck up at the boat and said, "There's snorkel gear in the big container up front, eh?"

"Really?"

Angus answered by deflating his vest and sinking beneath the surface.

Minutes later an excited Mikey splashed overboard. The water was surprisingly warm, and he soon caught up to the bubble trail that marked the path of the scuba diver. Mikey watched the Canadian hug the seafloor, ducking under rocky ledges and scratching about, raising clouds of sand.

Mikey floated overhead, mesmerized by the murky world. There were patterned fish and weird leafy plants and shells and sand snaking between the rocks like underwater arroyos. He spotted a large speckled stingray settling into the sand and was watching a fat turquoise fish chewing something from a rock when a shadow in his periphery caught his attention.

Heart spiking at the thought of a shark, he jerked his head around too fast, submerging the top of the snorkel and choking on seawater. He yanked out the mouthpiece and was coughing violently when he spotted the immense sea turtle drifting lazily into view. Its shell was ridged and blanketed with barnacles, the uneven edges draped with sea moss. Mikey kicked his flippers and saw a cluster of tiny fish darting back and forth beneath the expanse of its rigid belly. The slow-moving sea creature seemed no more interested in him than in the rocks below, and as it banked along the shoreline with the current, Mikey followed.

He noticed the stunted tail and the four wrinkled flaps that served as flippers, hardly moving yet effortlessly propelling the animal forward. The oddly patterned shell was etched with lines like a living, breathing puzzle. Mikey was surprised by the speed of the creature; he had to kick hard to keep pace with it. Its almond-shaped eyes were unblinking, supremely uninterested, as dark and black as onyx. Somehow, the school of minnows remained tight to its underbelly, never straying beyond the safety net of the shell.

Then, without warning, the turtle flapped all four of its flippers and was gone. Mikey squinted through his mask after it, confused. Nothing was different than it had been, and he hadn't moved aggressively. When he popped his head above the surface and looked around, his disorientation only deepened. The horizon was an endless expanse of blue. He turned his head and found the shoreline. He recognized the sea cave and wondered how he'd traveled so far from it. Then he noticed the rocks moving by and realized with a hot flush of panic that he was caught in a powerful current. Shading his eyes from the rising sun, he spotted the *pangas* and the sailboat far in the distance. His stomach dropped. He'd never make it against the current. The island was his only hope.

He'd started to kick toward shore when an explosion of bubbles startled him. He ducked his head beneath the surface and saw two heart-stopping images.

The first was his boss surging upward, the dive knife in his fist extending toward him.

The second was the mini-submarine—no larger than a Volkswagen Bug, a set of bloody fangs painted brightly on its side—tailing the suddenly homicidal Canadian.

CHAPTER FORTY-FIVE

Isla San Jose, Baja California Sur

At first Skegs thought nothing of the scuba diver hugging the outer ledge of the oyster reef—until he saw the man look up at the surface, free a large knife from his ankle sheath, and kick upward as if chased by a pack of moray eels.

That was when Skegs gazed up through the nose window of the submarine and saw the snorkeler.

He'd been staring down for almost an hour, surveying the oyster reef and reporting back to Fish and Toozie, who remained aboard the *Fish Goddess*. They'd arrived at the island just before dawn after transferring their squid-pecked prisoner to Santiago's skiff with instructions to deliver him to the authorities waiting at the Pichilingue ferry dock. Skegs had pressed to send the killer back down in the shark cage until Fish offered him the keys to the submarine and a first-class ticket to the oyster reef.

"And a pearl?" Skegs had inquired.

"We'll see," Fish had hedged.

"You're going to like the new paint job."

"The what?"

"Gave your underwater whirlybird a personality. Toughened her up a bit."

"You didn't."

Skegs beamed as he'd peeled back the canvas tarp and displayed his artwork. Then he'd called his La Paz friend and local *Federale*, Xavier, and reported the grisly crime at the apartment and the capture of the dive shop owner. He said the suspect was headed to the ferry dock at Pichilingue.

Before splitting up, Fish handed Santiago a roll of hundreds and an open invitation to Cantina del Cielo for all the free sand dab tostadas and double-baked tortillas he could eat, along with extra-large zip-ties from the toolbox to secure his captive for the short ride to the ferry dock.

Skegs slept after that—deep, restful sleep without worry of thugs with tire irons or a killer with mismatched eyes. Instead, his dreams were filled with underwater adventure worthy of Captain Nemo.

Now, seeing that the object of the knife-wielding scuba diver's aggression was his unlikely friend Mikey, Skegs flew into action. Somehow, the young fighter had not only escaped La Paz, but he was now snorkeling near the hidden oyster reef. Swimming on the surface, he was completely exposed to the glinting blade shooting up from the seafloor.

Sweeping aside a tsunami of questions, Skegs flipped the toggle switch engaging the sub's turbo drive and felt the craft surge into the current. Mikey had clearly seen his attacker, as he was now splashing desperately on the surface as his attacker fought his way up through the swift current, struggling not to overshoot his target.

Skegs felt his heart spike with adrenaline and dread. He knew the only way to save Mikey from the impending attack was to steer a path dangerously close to the surface. The current was working with the attacker and against the submarine, and even with the increased power, the timing had to be perfect. Skegs gave a short promise to Mechudo that the oysters would be saved and the pearls protected, and implored the spirit of the long-dead Indian boy to intervene to protect Mikey.

And then, in a voice that surprised him, Skegs promised, "And when I find my one and only pearl, it will go directly to the local church."

Mikey wasn't sure what would hurt worse, the slash of the knife or the collision with the hot-rod submarine. Tiring fast, he slowed and took a series of fast breaths, then ducked back beneath the surface. Maybe the vision had been a hallucination. After the last few days, he assumed anything was possible. But the submarine was real, and so was the pale-faced Canadian with murder in his eyes.

The submarine was flying up toward them, and Mikey saw with disbelief that the kidnapped Indian man he'd abandoned with his crazed ex-friends and a goggle-eyed psychotic was piloting it. Then his disbelief flashed to horror as the Indian swept the underwater craft deliberately into the knife-wielding scuba diver. There was a sudden blur of bubbles and blood, and then he saw the twisting shape of the Canadian swept away with the current, his limbs ghostlike in the shadowy water. The submarine had flashed out of sight.

Mikey rolled to his back, sucking at the fresh air and trying not to hyperventilate. The sun disappeared behind a cloud, and a sudden chill descended his spine. The current had him, and he could barely see the sailboat anchored in the distance. The trawler, too, was falling away with the island shoreline. Mikey had closed his eyes and was concentrating on slowing his heart, when the water next to him erupted with the hulk of the mini-submarine. The hatch opened and Skegs poked out his head.

"Need a lift?" the mescal salesman asked.

CHAPTER FORTY-SIX

Isla San Jose, Baja California Sur

Roscoe and Tawny moved fast. An hour earlier, from their lookout on the mountainous island, they'd watched the sun break like an egg over the eastern horizon. Then in the glare they watched a familiar trawler pull up to the island and drop anchor. Through the binoculars they followed the rich expatriate as he moved from the helm to the back deck, and then, to their amazement, uncover a miniature submarine painted to resemble a vampire fish. Moments later, the local Indian man who had promised to take them snook fishing appeared beside a set of winch controls and lowered the craft into the water.

"Double-crossers!" Roscoe spat, thrusting the binoculars into Tawny's hands. "Let's go get our pearl back!"

"Hang on a second," Tawny said, after raising the powerful glasses to her eyes. "Our pale-skinned sailor's suited up, and it looks like the younger guy's going in, too."

"So?"

"I know who the young guy is now."

"An old boyfriend?"

"Very funny. He was the one at the bar when those other two were thrown into the shark cage."

"The guy who got the faceful of lizard?"

Tawny nodded.

Roscoe grabbed for the binoculars and peered through the glass. "Holy crap." His jaw unhinged. "What the fuck's he doing here?"

Tawny grabbed their sleeping bags. "Time to roll."

Just as they rounded the island, they saw the little submarine burst through the surface beside the snorkeler about a hundred yards off. The hatch flew open, and in another moment the swimmer was hauled atop the nose cone by the pilot. Then the sub turned and motored along the surface toward the trawler, still anchored near the island.

Roscoe gunned the outboard and raced toward the big boat. The sub reached the trawler first and eased up to the stern. After Mikey slid from the nose cone to the dive step, Fish and Toozie opened the transom door and welcomed the young fighter aboard.

"Surprised to see you way out here, Mikey," Fish said.

"You know my name?" Mikey asked, shivering with exhaustion. He slumped to a knee.

Fish handed him a plastic squeeze bottle filled with orange liquid. "Your pal with the infection told me your name last time we spoke."

Mikey cringed at the memory of Tank's oozing scalp.

"You were caught in a hell of a current. Drink up before you get too dehydrated."

Mikey chugged half the bottle. "Damn, this is the best Gatorade ever," he said, wiping his lips with his forearm.

"It's not Gatorade—it's Tang," Fish said, and watched Toozie appear beneath the overhead cable and latch the clip to the ring plate of the submarine. "Astronauts used to drink it."

"Never heard of it," Mikey said, and finished the bottle.

Toozie moved to the control panel and brought the vessel aboard. Skegs waited for it to settle onto the chocks, and then climbed to the deck, favoring his injured ribs.

Mikey hurried to Skegs with his hand outstretched. "Thanks, man. I would have drowned."

Skegs ignored the hand and pulled the young fighter into a bear hug. "Or bled to death."

When Skegs released him, Mikey said, "He thought I was working with the locals. Not sure why, but I think it had something to do with sunken treasure."

A commotion on the other side of the boat caught their attention. They turned just as Roscoe banged the skiff into the dive step. "You stole our pearl!" he hollered with a raised fist.

Tawny rolled her eyes and waved a hand at Fish. "Permission to come aboard."

"Permission granted."

Mikey tossed a line to Roscoe, who caught it halfheartedly. He tied the skiff to the stern and waited for Tawny to disembark. Then he grabbed a fish bat and scrambled to her side.

"They played us," he growled, glaring at Fish and Skegs.

Tawny shook her head. "We don't know that. But even if they did, the pearls aren't ours to keep."

"They aren't theirs, either."

"Pearls?" Mikey blurted.

Skegs stepped forward. "This is all my fault," he explained to Roscoe. "The Canadian played *me*. Then he stole the pearl and burned down Fish's bar."

"He paid us to do it," Mikey interrupted. "I tried to talk them out of it, but they wouldn't listen. They were crazy mad about the cactus and the shark cage. And they were drunk."

Skegs looked at Mikey. "And the dive shop owner? How did he fit in?"

"The Canadian wanted dive gear. We found him in a bar. Grabbing you, though, was all Tank and Jimbo. I tried to reason with them, but by then I was an outsider."

"Yeah," Skegs said. "It was obvious they didn't trust you."

Smiling weakly, Mikey said, "But you were able to escape."

Skegs shrugged and drew a deep breath that sent his hands to his battered ribs. "Yeah, well, Mikey, I'm afraid Tank and Jimbo didn't."

Mikey's face drained of color.

"The dive shop owner killed them."

"Damn."

Skegs nodded. "We caught Crazy Eyes, anyway. He's heading to a Mexican jail for a very long time."

Tawny leaned heavily against the gunwale. "I wish we'd never found those pearls."

Fish said, "You didn't. Not really. Someone else found them, and lost them before appeasing the spirit of Mechudo."

"Mechudo?" Roscoe blurted. "What the hell is Mechudo? Sounds like that crappy soup they sell down here."

Skegs stifled a laugh. "He was a young diver who refused to give the first pearl he found to the church. He was drowned soon after by a giant clam. Then the oysters died out. Decades ago."

"The sailboat!" Tawny said, pointing.

In the distance, the fleet of *pangas* had converged en masse. One of the captains, an older man with a gray beard and a cast covering his arm, was boarding the unmanned boat.

"Zaragosa!" Fish exclaimed, and hurried to the helm. He engaged the anchor winch and fired the twin diesels, then turned the *Fish Goddess* toward the grouping of *pangas* and the crooked-masted sailboat.

Toozie joined Fish at the wheel while Skegs and Mikey moved into the boat's saloon for a change of clothes.

"As strange as it sounds," Skegs said, handing Mikey a dry Cantina del Cielo T-shirt from a stack tucked beneath the galley bar, "I'm sorry about your friends. They were assholes, but they didn't deserve to die."

Switching out of his wet shirt, Mikey asked, "How'd he do it?"

Skegs paused to consider Mikey's feelings. "How close were the three of you?"

Mikey wrapped a towel around his wet shorts and took a seat at one of the bar stools. "Tank was like my bodyguard growing up. He was funny, too. Everyone liked him. Then he started taking steroids and he got mean. Jimbo was just a workout partner. Tank liked him. I didn't."

"Tank never knew what hit him," Skegs lied. "Jimbo was a different story."

"Jimbo stayed too drunk to feel much of anything," Mikey commented. "How'd you get away?"

Skegs explained the transfer to the trunk of the Buick and his escape, and then the island and the shark cage and the squids.

"I've read about Humboldts," Mikey said with a shudder. "*National Geographic.* The way they attack scuba divers."

Skegs changed into a fresh shirt. "Little suckers have something like ten hearts and a bunch of fly eyes and piranha teeth in their tentacles. Zombielike fuckers capable of killing giant sperm whales."

"Three hearts," Mikey corrected.

"Yeah?" Skegs answered distractedly as he heard the engines slow and glanced through the galley windows. "Showtime."

As they exited the saloon, they heard Fish call out from the helm. At the gunwale railing, they found the pack of *pangeros* eyeing the exposed submarine as Fish descended the helm ladder. No one said a word.

Suddenly, a gray-bearded man appeared from the hatchway beneath the raised helm of the sailboat. He saw the trawler and smiled.

"*Hola, amigo,*" Zaragosa said with a wave. He climbed the short stairs and stepped to the deck. "You weren't kidding about the submarine. *Cómo está?*"

"*Bien,*" Fish replied. "This sailboat's been around since we left Magdalena Bay. The owner around?"

Before Zaragosa could reply, Skegs turned to Fish and said, "Long gone."

Fish gave his friend a questioning look, then glanced up at Toozie, who remained at the helm, idling the boat's engines. She only shrugged.

Skegs continued. "He ran into a little trouble underwater. Last I saw, he was drifting out to sea with the current. Quite dead, I can assure you."

Fish held Skegs's stare for a heartbeat, and then turned his attention back to Zaragosa to translate the news of the lost boat owner. Zaragosa reboarded his *panga,* showing little emotion.

"May I approach and tie off?" the old *pangero* asked.

"Of course," Fish said.

Zaragosa spoke to the group of *pangeros* before motoring to the stern of the trawler opposite the trailing skiff. After tying off on the remaining aft cleat, Zaragosa boarded with a youthful, bounding step. He explained in Spanish about the arrival of the sailboat and the ruse that got the pale-faced man to dive in the wrong spot. Then he explained about the arrival of the *pangeros* and the owner's idle threat with the gun. He stopped talking and pointed at Mikey, who stood listening at the door of the saloon. "Amigo," the old man said kindly, and explained how Mikey had communicated in Spanish, how they felt like they could trust the young man, who seemed more of a captive than a working deckhand.

"The sailboat is yours," Fish said. "Take it to La Paz and fix the mast and sell it. Share the money with these men who helped protect you."

Zaragosa shook his head, his eyes dancing with excitement. *"No necesita, señor."*

Fish looked confused until Zaragosa reached into the pocket of his overalls and then, grinning, held up the big pearl. He handed it to Fish. "This was in the soap dish. Mixed with sea glass. I almost missed it, but these old eyes will never forget the fire inside the belly of this one."

Fish was speechless. Toozie appeared at his side, and he handed her the deep red pearl with the crooked edges.

"My God," she said, holding the specimen in the sunlight, her eyes reflecting the pulse beating like a miniature heart.

Mikey stood frozen at the saloon door.

Tawny turned to Roscoe, whose mouth had gone bone-dry. "He's the one who lost them," she whispered.

Skegs stepped forward. *"El espíritu de Mechudo."*

Tawny elbowed Roscoe hard in the gut.

"Here," he said, unzipping his fanny pack and handing Zaragosa the two smaller pearls. "I believe these also belong to you."

Zaragosa accepted the pearls with a grateful countenance. Then he returned the favor. *"Para usted,"* he said, and handed Roscoe one of the two small pearls. *"La otra es para la iglesia."*

"No way!" Roscoe yipped. He looked around, embarrassed by his outburst. "And giving one to the church is cool, too."

"Damn straight," Skegs said.

Toozie returned the big pearl, and Zaragosa rolled them pleasurably in his rough hand.

Still beaming with excitement, Roscoe turned to Fish and patted him on the shoulder. "Sorry about my accusation. I didn't mean any harm."

"I know you didn't," Fish said.

"Please tell him we're glad he has them back."

Fish told Zaragosa this was the couple who had discovered the yellow bag caught on the barnacles. It reminded him of their visit to his bar in San Carlos, and their willingness to find the pearler who'd lost them.

Zaragosa turned to his benefactors. "Thank you," he said in heavily accented English. Then he pointed at the crooked-masted sailboat "I have no use for a sailboat. Take it." He waited as Fish translated, and then Zaragosa added in English, "Please."

Roscoe's eyes jitterbugged and his knees weakened. Tawny pulled Zaragosa into a tight hug. "Thank you."

Zaragosa's eyes misted. He pocketed the pearls with a nod of his head and turned to leave.

"*Vaya con Dios,*" Zaragosa said to Fish as he reboarded his *panga.* "All of us believe the oyster reef has returned for a reason. No one will dive it again. We must remain the caretakers of the pearls. For the future of our village and in honor of Mechudo." He grinned up at Fish. "Your support will, of course, be useful."

Fish returned his smile. "Plan on it, amigo. My amigo Skegs here will visit once a month with the stipend."

"*Gracias,*" Zaragosa said, and returned to his fellow *pangeros.*

"Excuse me," Mikey said, getting Fish's attention. "I'm truly sorry about your bar. I tried to stop them."

Fish stepped over and threw an arm around the young man's shoulders. "You threatened to burn it down, remember? Right before Mamacita hit you with the lizards."

Mikey's hand went to the scabs on his face. "I wasn't really going to do it. I just wanted Tank to think I would so you'd let them out of the cage."

"You got any skills other than punching cactus and hanging out with idiots?"

"I work construction to pay for college."

"You want a higher-paying job? It's temporary, but the boss pays all cash sans taxes. Room and board included."

Mikey blinked. "You mean here in Mexico?"

"I've got a cantina that needs rebuilding."

Mikey turned to Skegs, who grinned, then looked at Roscoe and Tawny and Toozie, all of whom were nodding happily.

Mikey turned back to Fish, eyes glassy with emotion. "Really?"

"Really."

Fish clapped him on the back and walked across the deck to where Toozie stood watching a lone dolphin slap the surface with its tail.

"Bottlenose telegraph," he said.

"It's so perfect here." Toozie sighed.

"I've been trying to buy this island for years. So it can remain perfect."

"It's privately owned?"

"Most of the islands are."

"You're a good man, Francis."

"Most people call me Atticus."

"You'll always be Francis to me."

"We're taking the boat back to Mag Bay. Want to come along for the ride? Meet a mule named Mephistopheles, hang out with a couple of iguanas forced onto the wagon while the bar gets rebuilt? As a bonus, you might even catch a black snook or two."

Toozie hesitated, and then slowly wagged her head. "I think I better hop off in La Paz on the way. I can catch a flight home from there."

Fish's hand went to his goatee. He stroked the braided chin hair and let his fingers linger on the metal crimp. "Are you making me chase you, Toozie?"

She smiled at him, but her eyes were thoughtful. "We have some things to sort out, you and I," she said. "Don't you agree?"

Fish let his sigh answer her. Yes, they had some things to sort out. Toozie was entangled in the wreckage of a past Fish had fled and generally succeeded in putting out of his mind. Except when his longing for the presence of this woman, and the girl they both loved, wrapped its tentacles around his heart. That longing squeezed so tightly now, he could barely whisper to her. "Tell me, Toozie. Would you rather I didn't chase you?"

It was her turn to sigh, but at least her smile fully inhabited her beautiful eyes now. "Chase away," she said. "But what makes you think I can be caught?"

"I like a challenge."

"As do I," she said, her tone sportive.

Fish's cheekbones lifted and his green eyes flashed. Then he dropped his hand from his goatee and clapped loudly. "The day's still young. Who wants a ride in a submarine?"

AFTERWORD

Pearls were big business in Baja California, and the pearl beds of La Paz were the most famous. For centuries, the local Pericú Indians dived for pearls, but by World War II, overharvesting and a devastating blight destroyed the beds. By the time John Steinbeck and Ed Ricketts sailed into the Sea of Cortez, most of the pearls were gone and the rich stories had become legends. They visited Isla San Jose, and Steinbeck's time there and in La Paz set the scene for his novella *The Pearl*. That little book had quite an impact on me and planted the seed for *The Crooked Pearl*.

In the last few years, rumors of pearl beds outside La Paz have begun to circulate. No one knows exactly where the pearls are, but the waters around Isla San Jose are suspect.

Red-hued pearls are a natural Sea of Cortez phenomenon, and yes, the Legend of Mechudo is well-known among locals. There is mention of it online for those interested in more research.

Pruning a cardón cactus may or may not aid in its recovery from a beating. I know it works for mesquites and palo verde trees, so why not cacti. I probably should have met with a cacti aficionado, but the logic of it swayed me. Isla San Jose is a remarkable island, immense and mesmerizing and beautiful beyond description. I've spent days fishing its shores and nights sleeping offshore aboard a small fishing boat. It is one of my favorite islands in the Sea of Cortez. And the village of San Evaristo is perfectly situated to access its prolific waters. But to get there takes patience and a vehicle with good tires. Whale sharks and orcas frolic in the passage between the village and this incredible island. You should visit someday.

I am a fan of the UFC. I hope Dana White appreciates my use of the three UFC wannabes. And I hope no real fighter ever takes on a cardón. He or she will lose.

Humboldt squids are one of the more unique creatures of the sea. They have three hearts and enormous camera-like eyes capable of reacting with precision to prey and predators alike. Fast and ferocious, they are armed with miniature sharklike teeth in each of their many suckers. They also have a parrotlike beak that can snap a fisherman's finger like a toothpick. They are nothing like an octopus.

My father nearly died in a sudden and unexpected *chubasco* like the one that capsized Zaragosa's panga. He, like Zaragosa, was fishing in the southern Sea of Cortez. Unlike Zaragosa, he was not confronted with a tsunami or an earthquake.

La Paz is not yet Cabo San Lucas, but all indications are that it soon may be. Which is a shame. Here's to hoping it holds out as long as possible.

Salud!

ACKNOWLEDGMENTS

As always, I am forever indebted to the kindness of Baja California's residents, both local and expatriate. Whether I am in La Paz or Puerto San Carlos or on some dirt road in between, they have always welcomed me with kindness. Thank you from the depths of my heart.

To John Steinbeck and Ed Ricketts who traveled to the Sea of Cortez back when marlin grew fat as steers and pearls were as abundant as seashells. What a thrill it must have been to cruise the Sea of Cortez aboard the seventy-five-foot *Western Flyer*. They set the groundwork for all the other Baja nomads to whom I am also indebted.

To my *compadres* and early readers, Captain Winston Warr III, Randy Denis, Mickey Morey, and Derek Crossley. Your friendships are precious, your insights priceless. Cheers. And an extra shout-out to Randy Denis for setting the scene with his hand-drawn maps.

To Tyler Dilts, author of *A King of Infinite Space* and *The Pain Scale*, who got me started on this novel path. An ocean of thanks, once again, my friend.

To my literary agent, Richard Pine. Your belief in this series has meant the world to me. The fish tacos are on me next time I'm in New York. And the Pacificos.

To Andrew Bartlett, Alan Turkus, Alison Dasho, and their team at Thomas & Mercer. A boatload of thanks only just begins to express my gratitude.

To David Downing whose editing skills are unmatched. Hugs, amigo. And thank you also to my copy editor, Jane Steele, whose fine-tuning took the salt off the gunwales and made the varnish shine.

And to Jacque Ben-Zekry and her tireless marketing team. A book is only as good as its readership. Thank you for getting the word out.

And lastly and most importantly to my muse, Amanda Trefethen. You challenge me to be a better writer, a better father, and a better husband. Love always and forever.

ABOUT THE AUTHOR

Shaun Morey is the author of the bestselling *Incredible Fishing Stories* series and a contributor to magazines and newspapers worldwide. He won the inaugural Abbey Hill short-story contest and is a three-time winner of the *Los Angeles Times* novel-writing contest. Over the years, he has worked as a fishmonger, a tennis instructor, a bartender, an associate literary agent, and an attorney—who could never quite figure out how to sue God and win—until he wrote *Wahoo Rhapsody*. Please visit www.shaunmorey.com for more information.